NINE MONTHS
TO REDEEM HIM

NINE MONTHS TO REDEEM HIM

BY

JENNIE LUCAS

First published in Great Britain 2015
by Mills & Boon, an imprint of Harlequin (UK) Limited,
Large Print edition 2015
Eton House, 18-24 Paradise Road,
Richmond, Surrey, TW9 1SR

ISBN: 978-0-263-25627-7

Harlequin (UK) Limited's policy is to use papers that
are natural, renewable and recyclable products and made
from wood grown in sustainable forests. The logging
and manufacturing processes conform to the legal
environmental regulations of the country of origin.

Printed and bound in Great Britain
by CPI Antony Rowe, Chippenham, Wiltshire

To Krystyn Gardner, my friend since childhood, maid of honor at my wedding—the bold, fearless soul who moved halfway round the world and convinced me to meet her there. Thanks, you crazy girl, for blazing a trail, and for always being in my corner.

PROLOGUE

THIS IS ALL I can give you, he said. *No marriage. No children. All I can offer is—this.* And he kissed me, featherlight, until I was holding my breath, trembling in his arms. *Do you agree?*

Yes, I whispered, my lips brushing against his. I hardly knew what I was saying. Hardly thought about the promise I was making and what it might cost me. I was too lost in the moment, lost in pleasure that made the world a million colors of twisting light.

Now, two months later, I'd just gotten news that changed everything.

As I went up the sweeping stairs of his London mansion, my heart was in my throat. *A baby.* I gripped the oak handrail as my shaking steps echoed down the hall. *A baby.* A little boy with Edward's eyes? An adorable little girl with his smile? Thinking of the sweet, precious baby soon to be nestled in my arms, a dazed smile lifted to my lips.

Then I remembered my promise.

My hands tightened. Would he think I'd somehow gotten pregnant on purpose? Tricking him into becoming a father against his will?

No. He wouldn't. Couldn't.

Could he?

The upstairs hallway was cold and dark. Just like Edward's heart. Because beneath his sensual charm, his soul was ice. I'd always known this, no matter how hard I'd tried *not* to know it.

I'd given him my body, which he wanted, and my heart, which he hadn't. Had I made the biggest mistake of my life?

Maybe he could change. I took a deep breath. If I could only believe that, once he knew about the baby, he might change—that he might someday love us both…

Reaching our bedroom, I slowly pushed open the door.

"You've kept me waiting," Edward's voice was dangerous, coming from the shadows. "Come to bed, Diana."

Come to bed.

Clenching my hands at my sides, I went forward into the dark.

CHAPTER ONE

Four Months Earlier

I WAS *DYING*.

After hours of being cooped up in the backseat of the chauffeured car, with the heat at full blast as the driver exceeded speed limits at every opportunity, the air felt oppressively hot. I rolled down the window to take a deep breath of fresh air and rain.

"You'll catch your death," the driver said sourly from the front. Almost the first words he'd spoken since he'd collected me from Heathrow.

"I need some fresh air," I said apologetically.

He snorted, then mumbled something under his breath. Pasting a smile on my face, I looked out the window. Jagged hills cast a dark shadow over the lonely road, surrounded by a bleak moor drenched in thick wet mist. Cornwall was beautiful, like a dream. I'd come to the far side of the world. Which was what I'd wanted, wasn't it?

In the twilight, the black silhouette of a distant crag looked like a ghostly castle, delineated against the red sun shimmering over the sea. I could almost hear the clang of swords from long-ago battles, hear the roar of bloodthirsty Saxons and Celts.

"Penryth Hall, miss." The driver's gruff voice was barely audible over the wind and rain. "Up ahead."

Penryth Hall? With an intake of breath, I looked back at the distant crag. It wasn't my imagination or a trick of mist. A castle was really there, illuminated by scattered lights, reflecting in a ghostly blur upon the dark scarlet sea.

As we drew closer, I squinted at the crenellated battlements. The place looked barely habitable, fit only for vampires or ghosts. For this, I'd left the sunshine and roses of California.

Blinking hard, I leaned back against the leather seat and exhaled, trying to steady my trembling hands. The smell of rain masked the sweet, slightly putrid scent of rotting autumn leaves, decaying fish and the salt of the ocean.

"For lord's sake, miss, if you've had enough of the rain, up it goes."

The driver pressed a button, and my window

closed, choking off fresh air as the SUV bumped over ridges in the road. With a lump in my throat, I looked down at the book still open in my lap. In the growing darkness, the words were smudges upon shadows. Regretfully, I marked my place, and closed the cover of *Private Nursing: How to Care for a Patient in His Home Whilst Maintaining Professional Distance and Avoiding Immoral Advances from Your Employer* before placing it carefully in my handbag.

I'd already read it twice on the flight from Los Angeles. There hadn't been much published lately about how to live on a reclusive tycoon's estate and help him rehabilitate an injury as his live-in physical therapist. The closest I'd been able to find was a tattered book I'd bought secondhand that had been published in England in 1959—and when I looked closer I discovered it was actually a reprint from 1910. But I figured it was close enough. I was confident I could take the book's advice. I could learn anything from a book.

It was *people* I often found completely unfathomable.

For the twentieth time, I wondered about my new employer. Was he elderly, feeble, infirm? And why had he sent for me from six thousand miles away? The L.A. employment agency had not been very forthcoming with details.

"A wealthy British tycoon," the recruiter had told me. "Injured in a car accident two months ago. He can walk but barely. He requested you."

"Why? Does he know me?" My voice trembled. "Or my stepsister?"

Shrug. "The request came from a London agency. Apparently he found the physical therapists in England unsuitable."

I gave an incredulous laugh. "*All* of them?"

"That's all I'm allowed to share, other than salary details. *That* is sizeable. But you must sign a nondisclosure agreement. And agree to live at his estate indefinitely."

I never would have agreed to a job like this three weeks ago. A lot had changed since then. Everything I'd thought I could count on had fallen apart.

The Range Rover picked up speed as we neared the castle on the edge of the ocean's cliff. Passing beneath a wrought iron gate carved into the shape of sea serpents and clinging vines, we entered a courtyard. The vehicle stopped. Gray stone walls pressing in upon all sides, beneath the gray rain.

For a moment, I sat still, clutching my handbag in my lap.

"'Consider a carpet,'" I whispered to myself, quoting Mrs. Warreldy-Gribbley, the author of the book. "'Be silent and deferential and endure, and expect to be trod upon.'"

I could do that. Surely, I could do that. How hard could it be, to remain silent and deferential and endure?

The SUV's door opened. A large umbrella appeared, held by an elderly woman. "Miss Maywood?" She sniffed. "Took you long enough."

"Um…"

"I'm Mrs. MacWhirter, the housekeeper," she said, as two men got my suitcase. "This way, if you please."

"Thank you." As I stepped out of the car, I looked up at the moss-laden castle. It was the first of November. This close up, Penryth Hall looked even more haunted. *A good place to heal*, I told myself firmly. But that was a lie. It was a place to hide.

I shivered as drops of cold rain ran down my hair and jacket. Ahead of me, the housekeeper waved the umbrella with a scowl.

"Miss Maywood?"

"Sorry." Stepping forward, I gave her an attempt at a smile. "Please call me Diana."

She looked disapprovingly at my smile. "The master's been expecting you for ages."

"*Master*..." I snorted at the word, then saw her humorless expression and straightened with a cough. "Oh. Right. I'm terribly sorry. My plane was late…"

She shook her head, as if to show what she thought of airlines' lackluster schedules. "Mr. St. Cyr requested you be brought to his study immediately."

"Mr. St. Cyr? That is his name? The elderly gentleman?"

Her eyes goggled at the word *elderly*. "Edward St. Cyr is his name, yes." She looked at me, as if wondering what kind of idiot would agree to work for a man whose name she did not know. A question I was asking myself at the moment. "This way."

I followed, feeling wet and cold and tired and grumpy. *Master,* I thought, irritated. What was this, *Wuthering Heights?*— The original novel, I mean, not the (very loosely) adapted teleplay that my stepfather had turned into a cable television miniseries last year, with a pouty-lipped starlet as Cathy, and so much raunchy sex that Emily Brontë was probably still turning in her grave. But the show had been a big hit, which just went to show that maybe I was every bit as naïve as Howard claimed. "Wake up and smell the coffee, kitten," he'd said kindly. "Sex is what people care about. Sex and money."

I'd disagreed vehemently, but I'd been wrong. Clearly. Because here I was, six thousand miles from home, alone in a strange castle.

But even here, between the old suits of armor and tapestries, I saw a sleek modern laptop on a table. I'd purposefully left my phone and tablet in Beverly Hills, to escape it all. But it seemed even here, I couldn't completely get away. A bead of sweat lifted to my forehead. I wouldn't look to see what they were doing, I *wouldn't…*

"In here, miss." Mrs. MacWhirter led me into a starkly masculine study, with dark wood furnishings and a fire in the fireplace. I braced myself to face an elderly, infirm, probably cranky old gentleman. But there was no one. Frowning, I turned back to the housekeeper.

"Where is—"

She was gone. I was alone in the flickering shadows of the study. I was turning to leave as well when I heard a low voice, spoken from the depths of the darkness.

"Come forward."

Jumping, I looked around me more carefully. A large sheepdog was sitting on a Turkish rug in front of the fire. He was huge and furry, and panting noisily, his tongue hanging out. He tilted his head at me.

I stared back in consternation.

Was I having some kind of breakdown, as my friend Kristin had predicted? I *had* seen enough funny pet videos online to know that animals could be trained to talk.

"Um." Feeling foolish, I licked my lips. "Did you say something?"

"Did I stutter?" The dog's mouth didn't move. So it wasn't the dog talking. But now I wished it had been. Animal voices were preferable to ghostly ones. Shivering, I looked around me.

"Do you require some kind of instruction, Miss Maywood?" The voice turned acid. "An engraved invitation, perhaps? Come forward, I said. I want to see you."

It was then I realized the deep voice didn't come from beyond the grave, but from the depths of the high-backed leather chair in front of the fire.

Oh. Cheeks hot, I walked toward it. The dog gave me a pitying glance, tempered by the faint wag of his tail. Giving the dog a weak smile, I turned to face my new employer.

And froze.

Edward St. Cyr was neither elderly nor infirm. No.

The man who sat in the high-backed chair was handsome, powerful. His muscled body was partially immobilized, but he somehow radiated strength, even danger. Like a fierce tiger—caged...

"You are too kind," the man said sardonically.

"You are Edward St. Cyr?" I whispered, unable to look away. I swallowed. "My new employer?"

"That," he said coldly, "should be obvious."

His face was hard-edged, rugged, too much so for conventional masculine beauty. There was nothing *pretty* about him. His jawline was square, and his aquiline nose slightly off-kilter at top, as if it had once been broken. His shoulders were broad, barely contained by the oversized chair, his right arm hung in an elastic brace in a sling. His left leg was held out stiffly, extended from his body, the heel resting on a stool. He looked like a fighter, a bouncer, maybe even a thug.

Until you looked at his eyes. An improbable blue against his olive-toned skin, they were the color of a midnight ocean swept with moonlight. Tortured eyes with unfathomable depths, blue as an ancient glacier newly risen above an arctic sea.

Even more trapped than his body, I thought suddenly. His soul.

Then his expression shuttered, turning sardonic and flat, reflecting only the glowing embers of the fire. Now his blue eyes seemed only ruthless and cynical. Had I imagined the emotion I'd seen? Then my lips parted.

"Wait," I breathed. "I know you. Don't I?"

"We met once, at your sister's party last June." His cruel, sensual lips curved. "I'm so pleased you remember."

"Madison is my *step*sister," I corrected automatically. I came closer to the chair, in the flickering light of the fire. "You were so rude…"

His eyes met mine. "But was I wrong?"

My cheeks burned. I'd been working as Madison's new assistant, so had been obligated to attend her posh, catered party. There'd been a DJ and waiters, and a hundred industry types—actors, directors, wealthy would-be producers. Normally I would have wanted to run and hide.

But this time, I'd been excited to bring my new boyfriend. I'd been so proud to introduce Jason to Madison. Then, later, I'd found myself watching the two of them, across the room.

A sardonic British voice had spoken behind me. *"He's going to dump you for her."*

I'd whirled around to see a darkly handsome man with cold blue eyes. *"Excuse me?"*

"I saw you come in together. Just trying to save you some pain." He lifted his martini glass in mocking salute. *"You can't compete with her, and you know it."*

It had been a dagger in my heart.

You can't compete with her, and you know it. Blonde and impossibly beautiful, my stepsister, who was one year younger, drew men like bees to a honeypot. But I'd seen the downside, too. Even being the most beautiful woman in the world didn't guarantee happiness.

Of course, being the ugly stepsister didn't guarantee it either. I'd glared at the man before I turned on my heel. *"You don't know what you're talking about."*

But somehow, he *had* known. It haunted me later. How had some rude stranger at a party seen the truth immediately, while it had taken me months?

When Madison arranged for Jason to get a part in her next movie, he'd been thrilled. Working as Madison's assistant, I'd seen them both every day on set in Paris. Then she'd asked me to go back to L.A. and give a magazine a personal tour of Madison's house in the Hollywood Hills, and talk about what it was like to be a "girl next door" who happened to have Madison Lowe as my stepsister, a semifamous producer as my stepfather, and up-and-coming hunk Jason Black as my boyfriend. "We need the publicity," Madison had insisted.

But the reporter barely seemed to listen as I walked her through Madison's lavish house, talking lamely about my stepsister and Jason. Until she pressed on her earpiece with her hand and suddenly laughed aloud, turning to me with a malicious gleam in her eye. *"Fascinating. But are you interested in seeing what the two of them have been up to today in Paris?"* Then she'd cut to reveal live footage of the two of them naked and drunk beneath the Eiffel Tower.

The video became an international sensation, along with the clip of my stupid, shocked face as I watched it.

For the past three weeks, I'd been trapped behind the gates of my stepfather's house, ducking paparazzi who wanted pictures of my miserable face, and gossip reporters who kept yelling questions like, *"Was it a publicity stunt, Diana? How else could anyone be so stupid and blind?"*

I'd fled to Cornwall to escape.

But Edward St. Cyr already knew about it. He'd even tried to warn me, but I hadn't listened.

Looking at my new employer now, a shiver went through me, rumbling all the way to my heart, shaking me like the earthquakes I thought I'd left behind. "Is that why you hired me? To gloat?"

Edward looked at me coldly. "No."

"Then you felt sorry for me."

"This isn't about *you*." His dark blue eyes glittered in the firelight. "This is about me. I need a good physiotherapist. The *best*."

Confused, I shook my head. "There must be hundreds, thousands, of good physical therapists in the U.K...."

"I gave up after four," he said acidly. "The first was useless. I hardly know which was thicker, her skull or her graceless hands pushing at me. She quit when I attempted to give her a gentle bit of constructive criticism."

"*Gentle?*"

"The second woman was giggly and useless. I sacked her the second day, when I caught her on the phone trying to sell my story to the press..."

"Why would the press want your story? Weren't you in a car accident?"

His lips tightened almost imperceptibly at the corners. "The details have been kept out of the news and I intend to keep it that way."

"Lucky," I said, thinking of my own media onslaught.

His dark eyes gleamed. "I suppose you're right." He glanced down at his arm in the sling, at his leg propped up in front of him. "I can walk now, but only with a cane. That's why I sent for you. Make me better."

"What happened to the other two?"

"The other two what?"

"You said you hired four physical therapists."

"Oh. The third was a hatchet-faced martinet." He shrugged. "Just looking at her curdled my will to live."

Surreptitiously, I glanced down at my damp cotton jacket, sensible nursing clogs and baggy khakis wrinkled from the overnight flight, wondering if at the moment, I too was curdling his will to live. But my looks weren't supposed to matter. Not in physical therapy. Looking up, I set my jaw. "And the fourth?"

"Ah. Well." His lips quirked at the edges. "One night, we shared a little too much wine, and found ourselves in bed in a totally different kind of therapy."

My eyes went wide. "You fired her for sleeping with you? You should be ashamed."

"I had no choice," he said irritably. "She changed overnight from a decent physio to a marriage-crazed clinger. I caught her writing *Mrs. St. Cyr* over and over on my medical records, circling it with hearts and flowers." He snorted. "Come *on.*"

"What bad luck you've had," I said sardonically. Then I tilted my head, stroking my cheek. "Or wait. Maybe *you're* the one who's the problem."

"There is no problem," he said smoothly. "Not now that you're here."

I folded my arms. "I still don't understand. Why me? We only met the once, and I'd already given up doing physical therapy then."

"Yes. To be an assistant to the world-famous Madison Lowe. Strange career choice, if you don't mind me saying so, from being a world-class physiotherapist to fetching lattes for your stepsister."

"Who said I was world-class?"

"Ron Smart. Tyrese Carlsen. John Field." He paused. "Great athletes, but notorious woman-izers. I'm guessing one of them must have given you reason to quit. Something must have made the idea of being assistant to a spoiled star sud-denly palatable."

"My patients have all been completely profes-sional," I said sharply. "I chose to quit physical therapy for—another reason." I looked away.

"Come on, you can tell me. Which one grabbed your butt?"

"Nothing of the sort happened."

"I thought you would say that." He lifted a smug eyebrow. "That's the other reason I wanted you, Diana. Your discretion."

Hearing him say he wanted me, as he used my first name, made me feel strangely warm all over. I narrowed my eyes. "If one of them had sexu-ally assaulted me, believe me, I wouldn't keep it a secret."

He waved his hand in clear disbelief. "You were also betrayed by your boyfriend and America's Sweetheart. You could have sold the story in an instant and gotten money and revenge. But you've never said a word against them. That's loyalty."

"Stupidity," I mumbled.

"No." He looked at me. "It's rare."

He made me sound like some kind of hero. "It's just common decency. I don't gossip."

"You were at the top of your profession in physical therapy. That's why you quit. One of your patients did something, didn't he? I wonder which—"

"For heaven's sake!" I exploded. "None of them did anything. They're totally innocent. I quit physical therapy to become an actress!"

Actress. The words seemed to echo in the dark study, and I wished I could take them back. My cheeks burned. Even the crackle of the fire seemed to be laughing at me.

But Edward St. Cyr didn't laugh. "How old are you, Miss Maywood?"

The burn in my cheeks heightened. "Twenty-eight."

"Old for acting," he observed.

"I've dreamed of being in movies since I was twelve."

"Why didn't you start sooner, then? Why wait so long?"

"I was going to, but…"

"But?"

I stared at him, then looked away. "It just wasn't practical," I mumbled.

Now he did laugh. "Isn't your whole family in the business?"

"I liked physical therapy," I said defensively. "I liked helping people get strong again."

"So why not be a doctor?"

"No one dies in physical therapy." My voice wobbled a little. I lifted my chin and said evenly, "It was a sensible career choice. I made a living. But after so many years…"

"You felt restless?"

I nodded. "I quit my job. But acting wasn't as fun as I thought it would be. I went on auditions for a few weeks. Then I quit that to become Madison's assistant."

"Your lifelong dream, and you only tried it for a few weeks?"

Looking down at my feet, I mumbled, "It was a stupid dream."

I waited for him to say, "There are no stupid dreams," or murmur encouraging or sympathetic noises, as people always did. Even Madison managed it.

"Probably for the best," Edward said.

My head lifted. "Huh?"

He nodded sagely. "You either didn't want it enough, or you were too cowardly to fight for it. Either way you were clearly headed for failure. Good to figure that out and quit sooner rather than later. Now you can go back to being useful. Helping me."

My mouth fell open. Then I glared at him.

"You don't know. Maybe I could have succeeded. You have some nerve to—"

"You waited your whole life to try for it, then quit ten minutes after you started? Give me a break. You're lying to yourself. It's not your dream."

"Maybe it is."

"Then what are you doing here?" He lifted a dark eyebrow. "You want to give it another shot? London has a thriving theater scene. I'll buy you the train ticket. Hell, I'll even send you back to Hollywood in my own jet. Prove me wrong, Diana." He tilted his head, staring at me in challenge. "Give it another go."

I stared at him furiously, hating him for calling my bluff. I wanted to grandly take him up on his offer and march straight out his front door.

Then I thought of the soul-crushing auditions, the cold reptilian eyes of the casting directors as they looked me over and dismissed me—too old, too young, too thin, too pretty, too fat, too ugly. Too worthless. I was no Madison Lowe. And I knew it.

My shoulders slumped.

"I thought so," Edward said. "So. You're out of a job and need one. Perfect. It just happens that I'd like to hire you."

"Why me?" I whispered over the lump in my throat. "I still don't understand."

"You don't?" He looked surprised. "You're the best at what you do, Diana. Trustworthy, competent. Beautiful…"

I looked up fiercely, suspecting mockery. *"Beautiful."*

"Very beautiful." His dark blue eyes held mine in the flickering light of the fire. "In spite of those god-awful clothes."

"Hey," I protested weakly.

"But you have qualities I need more than beauty. Skill. Loyalty. Patience. Intelligence. Discretion. Devotion."

"You make me sound like…" I motioned toward

the sheepdog on the rug. The dog looked back at me quizzically, lifting his head.

Edward St. Cyr's lips lifted at the edges. "Like Caesar? Yes. That's exactly what I want. I'm glad you understand."

Hearing his name, the dog looked between us, giving a faint wag of his tail. Reaching out, I scratched behind his ears, then turned back to glare at his master.

His master. Not mine.

"Sorry." I shook my head fiercely. "There's no way I'm staying to work for a man who wants a physical therapist he can treat like his dog."

"Caesar is a very good dog," he said mildly. "But let's be honest, shall we? We both know you're not going back to California, not with all the sharks in the water. You wanted to get away. You have. No one will bother you here."

"Except you."

"Except me," he agreed. "But I'm a very easy sort of person to get along with—"

I snorted in disbelief.

"—and in a few months, after I can run again, perhaps you'll have figured out what you truly want to do with your life. You can leave Penryth Hall with enough money to do whatever you want. Go back to university. Build your physical therapy business. Even audition." He shook his head. "Whatever. I don't care."

"You just want me to stay."

"Yes."

Helplessly, I shook my head. "I'm starting to think I might be better off just staying away from people."

His eyes glittered in the firelight. "I understand. Better than you might think."

I tried to smile. "Somehow I doubt a man like you spends much time alone."

He looked away. "There are all kinds of alone." He set his jaw. "Stay. We can be alone together," he said gruffly. "Help each other."

It was tempting. What was my alternative? And yet...

I licked my lips, coming closer to his chair near the fire. "Tell me more about your injury."

His handsome face shuttered as he drew back.

"Didn't the agency explain?" he said shortly. "Car crash."

"They said you broke your left ankle, your right arm and two ribs." I looked over his body slowly. "And also dislocated your shoulder, then managed to dislocate it *again* after you were home. Was it from physical therapy?"

He made a one-shouldered gesture that would have been a shrug. "I was bored and decided to go for a swim in the ocean."

He could have died. "Are you crazy?"

"I said I was bored. And possibly a little drunk."

"You are crazy," I breathed. "No wonder you got in a car accident. Let me guess. You were street racing, like in the movies."

The air in the dark study turned so chilly, the air nearly crackled with frost. His hand gripped the armrest, then abruptly released it.

"Got it in one," he said coldly. "I raced my car straight into a Spanish fountain and flipped it four times down a mountain. Exactly like a movie. Complete with the villain carted off in an ambulance as all the good people celebrate and cheer."

His friendliness had evaporated for reasons I didn't understand. Wondering what had really happened, I took a deep breath. "Too soon to joke about your accident, huh? Okay, got it." I bit my lip. "What really happened? What caused it?"

"I loved a woman," he said flatly. Jaw tight, he looked away, staring out the window. It was leaded glass, small-paned and looked very old. The last bit of reddish sun was dying to the far west.

"I find the topic boring." He looked at me. "How about we agree to forget about the past—both of us?"

It was the best plan I'd heard all day. "Deal."

"Jason Black sounds like an idiot in any case," he muttered.

The memory of Jason's warm eyes, his lazy smile, his sweet, slow Texas drawl—*Darlin', aren't you a sight for sore eyes*—made pain slice through me like a blade. Folding my arms tightly over my heart, I glared at my new employer. "Don't."

"So loyal," he sighed. "Even after he slept with your stepsister. Such devotion." Deliberately, he rested his eyes on his sheepdog, then turned back to me suggestively. I scowled.

"How do I know you won't toss me out tomorrow, for some trumped-up reason, like all the others?"

"I'll make you a promise." His dark blue eyes met mine. "If you'll make one to me."

As our eyes locked in the firelight, my whole body flashed hot, then cold. His deep, searing blue eyes made me feel strangely shivery. My gaze fell unwillingly to his mouth. His lips were sensual and wicked, even cruel.

And just the fact that I *noticed* his lips was a very bad sign. Mrs. Warreldy-Gribbley definitely would not approve.

Stay professional, she'd ordered in Chapter Six. *Keep your heart distant when you're physically close. Especially if your employer is handsome and young. Keep your touch impersonal and your voice cold. See him as a patient, as a collection of sinew and bone and spine, not as a man.*

Looking up, I said in a voice icy enough to flay the skin of a normal man, "You're not flirting with me, are you, Mr. St. Cyr?"

"Call me Edward." His eyes gleamed. "And no. I wasn't flirting with you, Diana." His husky voice made my name sound like music. I tried not to watch the flick of his tongue on his sensual lips with each syllable. "What I want from you is far more important than sex."

It had been an insane thing to worry about anyway—as if a gorgeous, brooding tycoon like Edward St. Cyr would ever look twice at a girl like me! "Oh. Good. I mean… Good."

"I need you to heal me. Whenever I'm not working. Even if it takes twelve hours a day."

"Twelve?" I said dubiously. "Physical therapy isn't an all-day kind of endeavor. We'd work together for an hour a day, maybe three at most. Not twelve…" I tilted my head. "What is your work?"

"I'm CEO of a global financial firm based in London. I'm currently on leave but a sizeable amount of work from my home office is still required. I'll need you available to me day or night, whenever I want you. I need you to be available for my therapy without question and without notice."

Dead silence followed, with only the crackling of the fire. Caesar the Sheepdog yawned.

I stared at Edward. "It's a completely unreasonable demand."

"Completely," he agreed.

"It would make me your virtual slave for months, possibly, at your beck and call, with no life of my own."

"Yes."

Considering the mess I'd made of my life myself, maybe that wouldn't be all bad. I looked at his leg, propped up on the stool. "Will you quit on me when it gets difficult?"

His shoulders stiffened. Putting his foot down on the floor, he used one hand to steady himself on the back of the chair, and slowly rose to his feet. He stood in front of me, and my head tilted back to look him in the eye. He was a foot taller. I felt how he towered over me, felt the power of his body like a broad shadow over my own.

"Will *you*?" he said softly.

I shook my head, looking away as I mumbled, "As long as you don't flirt with me."

"You have nothing to fear. My taste doesn't run to idealistic, frightened young virgins."

I whirled back to face him. "How did you—"

"I know women." His eyes were mocking as he looked down at me. He bared his teeth in a smile that glinted in the firelight. "I've had my share. One-night stands, weekend affairs—that is more my line. Sex without complications. That is how I play."

"Surely not since your accident—"

"I had a woman here last night." He gave his one-shouldered shrug. "An acquaintance of mine, a French lingerie model came down from London—we shared a bottle of wine and then we… But Miss Maywood, you look bewildered. I guessed you were a virgin but I expected you'd at least have *some* experience. Should I explain how it works?"

My face was probably the color of a tomato. "I'm just surprised, that's all. With your injury…"

"It's not difficult," he said huskily, looking down at me. "She sat on top of me. I didn't even have to move from my chair. I could draw you a diagram, if you like."

"N-no," I breathed. He was so close. I could almost feel the heat from his skin, the power from his body. He was right, I didn't have much experience but even I could see that this man was dangerous to women. Even idealistic young virgins like me.

Edward St. Cyr was the kind of man who would break your heart without much bothering about it. Casually cruel, like a cat toying with a mouse.

"So you agree to the terms?"

Hesitantly, I nodded. He took my hand. I nearly gasped as I felt the warmth of his skin, the roughness of his palm against mine. A current of electricity went through me. My lips parted.

"Good," he said softly. We were so close, I smelled his breath, warm and sweet—like liquor. I saw his bloodshot eyes. And I realized, for the first time, that he was slightly drunk.

A half-empty bottle of expensive whiskey was

on the table by his chair, beside a short glass. Dropping his hand, I snatched them up. "But if I'm going to stay and be on call for you every hour of the day, you're going to commit as well. No more of this."

His dark eyebrow raised. "It's medicinal."

I didn't change my tone. "No drugs of any kind, except, if you're very nice to me, coffee in the morning. And no more late nights with lingerie models."

Edward smiled. "That's fine."

"Or anyone else!" I added sharply.

He scowled, folding his arms like a sulky boy. "You're being unreasonable."

"Yes," I agreed. "So that makes two of us."

"But if you take away all my toys, Diana," he looked me over, "what else will I have to play with?"

My cheeks burned at his deliberately insulting glance. "You'll have hard work," I said crisply, "and lots of it."

Edward leaned back, his handsome face cold. "You still yearn for Jason Black."

The cruelty of his words hit me like a blow. With an intake of breath, I looked towards the window at the deepening night. I saw my plain reflection in the glass, against the red-orange glow of the fire.

"Yes," I whispered, and was proud my voice held steady.

"You lo-ove him," he said mockingly.

My throat choked. Madison and Jason were probably making love right now, in their elegant suite at a five-star Parisian hotel. I said in a small voice, "I don't want to love him anymore."

"But you do." He snorted, looking over me with contemptuous eyes. "You'll probably forgive that stepsister of yours, too."

"I love them." I sounded ashamed. And I was. What kind of idiot loves people who don't love her back? My teeth chattered. "People…can't choose who they l-love."

"My God. Just look at you." Edward stared at me for a long moment. "Even now, you won't say a word against them. What a woman."

Silence fell. The wind howled outside, shaking the leaded glass in the thick gray stone.

"You're wrong, you know," he said quietly. "You *can* choose who you love. Very easily."

"How?"

"By loving no one."

At those breathtakingly cynical words, I looked

at his powerful, injured body. The hard jaw, the icy blue eyes. Edward St. Cyr was the master of Penryth Hall, handsome and wealthy beyond imagining.

He was also damaged. And not just his body.

"You've had your heart broken too," I whispered, searching his gaze. "Haven't you?"

Edward looked me over in a way that caused my body to flash with heat. He took a step closer, and his muscular, powerful body towered over me in every direction.

"Perhaps that's the real reason I wanted you here," he murmured. "Perhaps we are kindred spirits, you and I. Perhaps we can—" he brushed back a tendril of my hair "—heal each other in every way…."

Edward pulled closer to me. I felt the warmth of his breath against my skin and shivered all over. My heart was beating frantically. He started to lower his head toward mine.

Then I saw the sardonic twist of his lips.

Putting my hands on his chest—on his hard, muscular, delicious chest, warm through his shirt—I said, "Stop it."

"No?" Taking a step back, laughing, he mocked me with my earlier words. "Too soon?"

"You are *a jerk*," I choked out.

He shrugged his one-shoulder shrug. "Can't blame me for trying. You seem so naïve, like you'd believe any line a man told you." He considered me. "Kind of amazing you're still a virgin."

Outrage filled me, and new humiliation. "You claim you're desperate to be healed—"

"I never used the word *desperate*."

"Then you fire your physical therapists, and waste your days getting drunk—"

"And don't forget my nights having sex," he said silkily.

"You're already trying to sabotage *me*." Narrowing my gaze, I lifted my chin. "I don't think you actually *want* to get better."

His careless look disappeared and he narrowed his eyes in turn. "I'm hiring you as a physio, Miss Maywood, not a psychiatrist. You don't know me."

"I know I came a long way here to have my time wasted. If you don't intend to get better, tell me now."

"And you'll do what? Go back home to humiliation and paparazzi?"

"Better that, than be stuck with a patient who

has nothing but excuses, and blames others for his own laziness and fear!"

"You say this to my face?" he growled.

"I'm not afraid of you!"

Edward stared at me blankly.

"Maybe you should be." He fell back heavily into the chair and stared at the fire. The sheepdog lifted his head, wagging his tail.

"Is that what you want?" I said softly, coming closer. "For people to be afraid of you?"

The flickering firelight cast shadows on the leatherbound books of his starkly masculine study. "It makes things simpler. And why shouldn't they fear me?" His midnight-blue eyes burned through me. "Why shouldn't you?"

Edward St. Cyr's handsome face and cultured voice were civilized, but that was a veneer, like sunlight over ocean. Beneath it, the darkness went deeper than I'd imagined. In spite of my earlier brave words, something shivered in my heart, and I suddenly wondered what I'd gotten myself into.

"Why should I be afraid of you?" I gave an awkward laugh. "Is your soul really so dark?"

"I loved a woman," he said in a low voice, not looking at me. "So much I tried to kidnap her from her husband and baby. That's how I got in the accident." His lips turned flat. "Her husband objected."

"This is why you wouldn't allow the agency to give me any details," I said slowly, "not even your name. You were afraid if I knew more about you, I wouldn't come, weren't you?"

His jaw tightened.

"Was anyone hurt?"

His expression suddenly looked weary. "Only me."

"And now?"

"I've left them to their happiness. I've found that love, like *dreams,*" he said the word mockingly, "offers more pain than pleasure." He turned to me in the firelight, his expression stark. "You want to know about the depths of darkness in my soul?" His lips twisted. "You couldn't even see it. You, who are nothing but innocence and sunlight."

I frowned at him. "I'm more than that." I suddenly remembered my own power, what I could do. The glimmer of fear disappeared. "I can help you. But you must promise to do everything I say. Everything. Exercises, healthy diet, lots of sleep—all of it." I lifted an eyebrow. "Think you can keep up with me?"

His lips parted. "Can *you* keep up with me? I've broken a lot of physiotherapists," he said dryly. "What makes you think I can't break you? I…" He suddenly scowled. "What are you smiling at? You should be afraid."

I *was* smiling. For the first time in three weeks, I felt a sense of purpose, even anticipation as I shook my head. The high-and-mighty tycoon didn't know who he was dealing with. Yes, I was a pathetic pushover in my personal life. But to help a patient, I could be as ruthless and unyielding as the most arrogant hedge fund billionaire on earth. "You are the one who should be afraid."

"Of you?" He snorted. "Why?"

"You asked for all my attention."

"So?"

My smile widened to a grin. "Now you're going to get it."

CHAPTER TWO

"YOU CALL THIS a workout?" Edward demanded the next morning.

I gave him a serene smile. "Those were just tests. Now we're about to start."

We were in the former gardener's cottage, which Edward had recently had converted into a personal rehabilitation gym, complete with exercise equipment, weight benches, yoga mats and a massage table, with big bright windows overlooking the garden. I had him lift his arms slowly over his head, saw the pull in his muscle, saw him flinch.

"Okay." I squared my shoulders. "Let's begin."

Then started the stretches and small weights and balancing and walking and then driving him to the nearest town recreation area so he could swim. I nearly brought him to his knees, literally as well as figuratively. I think I surprised him by pushing him to his limit, until he was covered with sweat.

"Ready to be done?" I said smugly.

Now he surprised me, by shaking his head. "Done? I'm just getting started," he panted. "When will the real workout begin?"

Leaving me to grit my teeth and come up with exercises that would continue to strengthen him, or at least not cause him injury.

As the afternoon faded into early evening, he never once admitted weakness or exhaustion. It was only by the grip of his fingers and the ashy-pale hue of his skin that I knew.

On the second day, though, I knew he'd be sore. I expected him to plead the demands of business, and spend his day with ice packs on his aching muscles, relaxing in his home office and talking on the phone. But when I told him to meet me in the gardener's cottage after breakfast, he didn't complain. And when I went down to set up, I found Edward already at the weight bench, lifting a heavier weight on his shoulder than he should have.

"Linger over your kippers and eggs, did you?" he said smugly. And then the second day went pretty much like the first, except this time it felt like he was a step ahead.

So the third day, determined to regain a sense of control, I had an early breakfast and went down to the gardener's cottage, at nine. I was able to greet his surprised face when he arrived five minutes later.

The fourth day, he was already there stretching when I arrived at eight forty-five.

We fell into a pattern. Any time Edward wasn't working in his home office, on his computer or the phone at odd hours talking to London, New York, Hong Kong and Tokyo, he demanded my full attention. And as promised, he got it. Each of us trying to prove we were tougher than the other. A battle of wills, neither of us willing to back down.

And now, almost two months into our working together, it had come down to this.

I'd woken up at five this morning, cursing myself in the darkness, when any sensible person would have drowsed in bed for hours longer. I'd been woken by Caesar, who'd trotted into my bedroom to heft his huge fluffy body at the foot of my bed. The sheepdog had become my morning alarm, because he only came to visit me after Edward was gone. When the dog woke me, I knew the day's battle was already half-lost.

Now, snow was falling softly outside as I hurried toward the gardener's cottage. I pulled the hood of my sweatshirt more tightly over my head, shivering as the gravel crunched beneath my feet. It was still dark, as was to be expected at five o'clock in December, the darkest day of the year.

I'd thought I could bring Edward St. Cyr to his knees? Ha. I'd thought I would make him beg for mercy? Double ha.

I'd worked with football players, injured stuntmen, even a few high-powered corporate types. I thought I knew what to expect from the typical arrogant alpha male.

But Edward was tough. Tougher than I'd ever seen.

Shivering down the garden path in the darkness, I pushed open the cottage door to discover that, just as I'd thought, Edward was already there. Doing yoga stretches on the mat, he looked well warmed up, his skin glowing with health, his body sleek in the T-shirt and shorts as he leaned forward in Downward Dog. My eyes lingered unwillingly on his muscular backside, pushed up in the air.

"'Morning." Straightening, Edward looked back at me with amusement, as if he knew exactly where my eyes had been. I blushed, and his grin widened. He stretched his arms over his head, then spread his arms and legs wide in Warrior II Pose. "Enjoy your lie-in, did you?"

"I didn't sleep in," I protested. "It's the middle of the night!"

He lifted his eyebrows and murmured, "If five is too early for you, just say so."

I glared at him. "It's fine. Happy to be here." I'd come at four tomorrow, I vowed privately. Maybe I'd start sleeping in the gym, instead of the beautiful four-poster bed down the hall from Edward's master suite on the second floor of Penryth Hall.

Edward looked at me with infinite patience. "Whenever you're ready...."

Scowling, I stomped to the equipment closet, where I yanked out a stairstep and some resistance bands. The bands got caught, so I yanked even harder.

"Maybe you should do some yoga," he observed. "It's very calming."

My scowl deepened. "Let's just get started."

I supervised his stretches, rotating his foot and his arm and shoulder, before we progressed to squats and knee lifts on the step, then thirty minutes on the exercise bike, then stretching again with the resistance bands, then walking on the treadmill, then lifting weights—carefully, with me spotting him. I helped him stretch and strengthen his muscles, stopping him before he could do himself another injury, or dislocate his shoulder again. But it was a constant battle between us. He worked like a demon at it, and his determination showed.

After nearly two months, he no longer wore a sling or brace. In fact, looking at him now, you wouldn't see a sign of injury. He looked like a powerful, virile male.

And he was.

Damn it.

Don't notice. Don't look.

We'd become almost friends, in a way. During the hours of physical therapy, we'd talked to fill the silence, and prove that neither of us was winded. I'd learned that his financial firm was worth billions, was called St. Cyr Global, and had been started by his great-grandfather, then run by his grandfather and father, until Edward took it over at twenty-two with his father's death. He'd tried to explain what his company did precisely, but it was hopeless. My eyes glazed faster than you can say *derivatives* and *credit default swaps*. It was more interesting to hear him talk about his cousin Rupert, whom he hated, his rival in the company. "That's why I need to get better," he said grimly. "So I can crush him."

Seemed a strange way to treat family. When I was ten, my beloved father had died, which had been gut-wrenching and awful. A year later, my mom had married Howard Lowe, a divorced film producer with a daughter a year younger than me. Howard's outlandish personality was a big change from my father's, who'd been a gentle, bookish professor, but we'd still been happy. Until I was seventeen, and my mom had gotten sick. Afterward, I'd realized I wanted a career where I could help people. And patients never died.

"You've never lost a single one?" Edward said teasingly.

"You might be the first," I'd growled. "If you don't quit adding extra weights to your bar."

But there were some topics we carefully avoided. I never mentioned Madison, or Jason or my failed movie career. We never again discussed Edward's car accident in Spain, or the woman he'd loved and tried to kidnap from her husband. We kept it to two types of talk—small and smack.

We'd become coworkers, of a sort. Friends, even.

Friends, I thought mockingly. *He's a client. Not a friend.*

So why did my body keep noticing him not as a patient, not even as a friend—but a man?

Beneath the rivalry and banter, I felt his eyes linger on me. I told myself not to take it personally. I'd cut him off from his sex supply. It was like denying gazelles to a lion. He was hungry. And I was handy. He couldn't help himself from looking, but I wouldn't fall prey to it.

And so I kept telling myself as we worked together in near silence, till the sun rose weakly over the horizon. Then I heard his stomach growl.

"Hungry?" I said in amusement.

Straightening from his stretch, he looked at me. "You know I am," he said quietly.

I turned away, trying to ignore the sudden pounding of my heart. I tried to think of what Mrs. Warreldy-Gribbley would say. Looking at my watch, I kept my voice professional. "Time for breakfast."

But I couldn't stop looking at him beneath my lashes as we left the cottage to go back to the hall. Edward was so darkly handsome. So powerful and dangerous. So everything that Jason was not.

Stop it. Don't think that way. But I shivered as we tromped through the snowy garden, beneath morning skies that had now turned sodden violet in color.

A full English breakfast, prepared by Mrs. Mac-Whirter, was soon ready for us in the medieval dining hall. As I sat beside Edward at the end of the long table, I watched his hands pour hot tea into his china cup. I felt hyperaware of his every movement as he served himself bacon and eggs and toast. I felt him lift the fork to his mouth. I could almost wish I was bacon, feeling the caress of his breath and tongue.

This was getting ridiculous.

Shaking myself angrily, I dumped a bunch of cream and sugar into my coffee.

I couldn't let myself linger over the face and body of my handsome, brooding boss. But I couldn't stop. For weeks, my eyes had lingered over his chiseled jawline, often dark with five o'clock shadow. Lingered over the curve of his cruelly sensual lips. Over his wicked smile. Over his large hands, the thickness of his neck, his muscled forearms, dusted with dark hair.

And his eyes. When they met mine, I lingered there most of all.

As I sat next to him now at the breakfast table, pretending to read the newspaper, I couldn't stop being aware of everything about him. Every time he moved, every slight vibration from his direction amplified in waves. When the waves hit my body, they could have been measured on the Richter scale.

Sadly, there was no chapter in Mrs. Warreldy-Gribbley's book about how a nurse should quash her own lust.

Lust. I shivered. Such an ugly word, without love to make it pretty. Because I knew I didn't love him. I saw the darkness in his soul too acutely. He trusted no one, cared for no one. Especially not the women he'd taken to his bed. If he had cared for any of them, he would have written or called her. Instead, there was nothing. If he couldn't take a woman to bed, he wasn't going to bother with her. It was despicable, really.

But my hand still shook as I held my coffee cup. If he knew how easily he could seduce me...

Edward St. Cyr was a powerful man accustomed to satisfying his every desire. Sex-starved as he was, he might make short work of me right here, on this table. He'd lick me like salty bacon, pull me into his mouth like the sweet, plump imported strawberries. He'd satiate himself quickly with the offered treat—my body—and forget me an hour later. Just like what he was eating now....

Desperate for distraction, I snatched up the London newspaper he'd just finished. Edward looked up with a frown. "Wait—"

His warning was too late. As I opened the page, I saw a picture of Madison on a red carpet, smiling in a glamorous sequined gown as she attended the premiere of her latest blockbuster in Leicester Square. At her side, slightly behind her in a tuxedo, was Jason.

"Oh," I breathed, and even to my own ears it sounded like a choked, bewildered wheeze, the sound someone makes when they'd just been punched.

Something grabbed my hand. Blinking hard, I saw it was Edward's hand, holding mine tightly over the table. Was he trying to comfort me?

Abruptly, he dropped his hand. Lifting a sardonic eyebrow, he looked at the photo. "He looks like a trussed duck," he observed.

"She's dragging him behind her like a baby blanket."

"You're wrong," I said automatically, then looked more carefully. Hmm. Now that Edward had pointed it out, Jason did look rather like an accessory, rather than a man, as Madison clutched his hand, dragging him behind her.

"And that white toothy smile of his," Edward continued, rolling his eyes. "How much did he pay for those?"

"His smile is lovely!" I protested.

"The white hurts my eyes." He briefly covered them. "I've never seen anything so fake."

"Shut up!"

"Right. I forgot he's your dream man." Leaning back in the chair, Edward took a gulp of his black tea as he rolled his eyes. "See where love gets you."

For about the hundredth time, I wondered about the woman who had broken his heart in Spain. The one who'd made him care so much that he'd actually tried to kidnap her. What had been so special about her? I looked back down at the photo of my stepsister and Jason, beaming at the camera.

See where love gets you...

I set down my fork. "Let's get back to work." I tilted my head and said challengingly, "Unless you need a longer break..."

Edward's cup fell with a clatter against the saucer. His eyes were gleaming with the joy of the fight. "I've been ready for ten minutes. I was waiting for you."

An hour later, back at the cottage, he was walking on the treadmill at the slow speed he hated.

"This is boring," he grumbled.

"It's fine," I insisted.

"No." He turned up the treadmill speed.

"Don't!" I said sharply.

He turned it up even more.

"You're going to kill yourself!" Then my eyes went wide as I drew back, watching him—this man who at the beginning of November had walked with a cane—now jogging forcefully on the treadmill. Edward had improved more rapidly than any client I'd ever seen.

"It's almost superhuman," I breathed. I jumped when I realized I'd said it out loud. Praise wasn't part of our deal. I blushed. "I, um, mean…"

"No. I heard you perfectly." Still jogging, Edward turned his head to give me a triumphant grin. "I *amaze* you with my strength and power. You're in *awe*. You're wishing right now you could give me a *big fat kiss*...."

"Am not!" I said indignantly, my cheeks on fire.

"I can see it in your face." His grin widened. "*Oh Edward*," he said mockingly in falsetto,

"You're incredible. You're my own personal hero—"

His sentence ended when his ankle abruptly twisted beneath him. He slammed down hard, cracking his shoulder and head against the treadmill. In a second, I was on my knees beside him.

"Are you all right?" Luckily he'd been wearing the safety, which made the treadmill's engine stop, or the skin of his cheek would have been ripped raw. "Careful. Don't sit up so fast—"

Ignoring me, he ripped his arm away with a scowl. "I'm fine."

"It was my fault—"

"It wasn't," he said shortly.

"I distracted you."

Edward looked even more ticked off than ever. "Stop trying to take the blame. You didn't do anything."

"Your head's bleeding. We might need to take you to a hospital—" But as I started to run my hands along his head, he yanked away.

"Stop bothering. I said I'm fine." He put his hand to his scalp and his skin was covered in blood as he pulled it away.

Rushing across the cottage, I grabbed a clean white towel. Turning on the hot water in the sink,

I got it wet and soapy then brought it back to him. Taking it without comment, he wiped his head. I put my hands over my mouth, almost ill with guilt.

"I shouldn't have let you push yourself so hard. It's my job to control you.…"

"As if you could," he gibed. He snorted, and one corner of his lips lifted as he looked at me. "Seriously. Think about it."

Our eyes met. My shoulders relaxed slightly.

"That's true. I can't tell you anything, can I?"

He shook his head. "Not a thing."

Seeing the blood dripping down his forehead, my smile fell. "But you can't be strong all the time, Edward." My voice faltered. "Even you have moments of weakness.…"

His smile changed to a glare. "*Weakness?*"

I recoiled from the blast of cold anger. "From your injury."

"Ah. Well. That's what I'm paying you for, isn't it?" He bared his teeth into a smile. "To wipe every trace of weakness from my body, to make me twice the man I was before she—"

He looked away, his jaw tight.

"Do you miss her?" I said softly.

"No," he bit out. He pulled the towel from his

head. "She was a good reminder of the lesson I learned as a child. Never depend on anyone."

What had happened when he was a child? I wondered. "You depend on *me*."

"To fix me? Yes. To keep my secrets? Yes."

"That's something, isn't it?"

"Yes," he said slowly, looking at me. "That's something." He abruptly turned away. Grabbing the handrail of the treadmill, he pulled himself to his feet. "The bleeding's stopped. Back to work."

"You're going to run more?" I stared at him in shock.

"Why not, are you tired?" he said challengingly.

I held up my hands. "Don't even! You're going to hurt yourself!"

"I know what I can handle." But as he stepped back on the treadmill, I saw the white of his knuckles as he gripped the handrails.

Edward was used to commanding everything and everyone. He was nearly killing himself to prove his strength. And forget the time a few thousand pounds of steel had crushed him like a blade of grass.

"A body needs time to heal." I put my hand over his. "Even a body like yours."

He tilted his head with a mocking smile. "Looking, were you?"

I blushed. "No. That is, yes, of course I was, but—"

"I like it when you blush." Turning away, he reached for the power button of the treadmill. He really was determined to kill himself.

"No more running for today," I said desperately. What could I possibly do to stop him? "Um—take off your clothes and lie down."

He gave a low laugh. "You really don't want me to run. Very well," he said gravely. "If you're determined to lure me away with sex, I accept."

"Take your clothes off for a *massage*. I don't want you to stiffen up...." The corners of his lips quirked, and I scowled. "Shut *up!*"

"I didn't say anything," he said meekly.

I pointed at the massage table. "You know what I want."

"Yes, as a matter of fact I do." Stepping off the treadmill, Edward looked down at me with a gleam of light in his eyes. "I'm just surprised it's taking you so long to admit it."

He was so close. And looking at me so intensely. My heart was pounding. All he had to do was reach out and take me in his arms.

"Admit what?" I breathed, trying to ignore the bead of sweat between my breasts as heat flashed through me. "Admit you're a colossal pain?"

"Have it your way." With a grin, he stepped back and reached up to pull his T-shirt off his body. "So you want me naked, huh? I knew sooner or later you'd be begging me to—" He flinched, and exhaled, dropping his arms. Gritting his teeth, he started to try again.

"Stop. Is it your shoulder?"

"It's fine," he ground out, an obvious lie. He must have hit his shoulder harder than I'd thought.

Coming to him, I ran my hands over his shoulder anxiously, then exhaled. "It's not dislocated."

"I told you." He started to reach up to pull off his shirt.

"Stop. Let me do it."

He tilted his head, his eyes gleaming. "Be my guest."

My hands shook as I lifted his faded cotton T-shirt upward, trying to ignore the warmth and steel of his tautly muscled chest and shoulders beneath my fingertips. I yanked it over his head, tousling his dark hair that my fingers longed to touch, to see if it was as silky as it looked.

He straightened. "Thanks."

"No problem." I couldn't stop my eyes from lingering over his hard-muscled form laced with dark hair. I licked my lips.

Then our eyes met.

Our bodies were still so close together. The upper half of his body was now naked.

And Edward suddenly smiled.

Not a friendly smile. A dangerous one, full of masculine power that threatened all kinds of things. Things I would like. Things that would pleasure my body. Things that would break my heart.

But I'd already had my heart broken once. And if Jason Black had broken it, Edward St. Cyr would crush it, smash it, light it on fire and then laugh, as he watched the ashy remains float softly to the ground.

"Are you going to take off the rest of my clothes, or shall I?" His dark sapphire eyes gleamed. "It might assist in your massage to take off your own clothes as well."

A selfish man may try to tempt the unwary virgin into sensual pleasures beyond her imagining, Mrs. Warreldy-Gribbley had warned. *There is only one means of resistance. The weapon of icy courtesy.*

Coldly, I lifted my chin. "This isn't a *date*. Your muscles need to be massaged after all your exercise today, and the fall. Otherwise you'll hurt." Grabbing a large white towel, I flung it at him. "Don't lift your shoulder again today. Let me know when it's safe to turn around."

Folding my arms, I turned the opposite direction. Furious at myself.

Why did I let him have this effect on me? No other client, and there had been some good-looking ones, had remotely made me feel like this. Even Jason had never made me feel like this. The times he'd kissed me had been pleasant. But he'd never made me feel so confused, off-kilter, and well, *burning hot*....

"You can turn around."

I did so. And wished I hadn't.

Edward was stretched naked, facedown across the massage table, as I'd ordered, covered only by a white towel across his backside, between his powerful back, his slender hips and thickly muscled thighs. Leaning his elbow against the leather cushion of the table, he propped up his head and looked at me darkly.

"Isn't this what you wanted?" he said huskily. "Me naked and at your mercy?"

I opened my mouth for a witty comeback, but only a squeak came out. I coughed to cover, then nervously went to the table. *It's no big deal,* I told myself fiercely. I'd massaged him many times over the past few weeks.

But something felt different. Something had changed. My skittish sexual awareness of him had managed to penetrate the gym. Why? How?

Edward lifted a dark eyebrow. "Be gentle with me," he said mockingly. Closing his eyes, he propped his chin on his folded arms and waited for me to touch him.

Touch him.

I looked down at my hands, which felt suddenly tingly. I knew how to give a professional massage. Why were my hands shaking? I didn't feel like a competent physical therapist. I felt like what he'd once called me—a frightened virgin.

Edward St. Cyr, my boss who'd inspired me and irritated me in equal measure, who was way out of my league and didn't see me as anything more than someone he could casually flirt with, and perhaps casually sleep with, and casually forget, was naked beneath my hands. And I feared if I showed a moment of weakness, he might roll over and devour me. I pictured a lion devouring a gazelle in a documentary, the flashing jaws digging into the meat and sinew.

If he felt my hands shaking… All he had to do was turn around on the table and pull me down hard against him in a savage kiss.

Don't think about it, I told myself fiercely. Flexing my fingers, I poured oil in one palm then rubbed my hands together to warm them. Slowly, I lowered them to his back.

Edward's skin was warm, like satin. I heard the soft whir of the nearby space heater as I ran my hands down the length of his spine, feeling the smoothness of his skin over hard muscle.

I wondered what his naked body would feel like, pressed against my own.

Muscles. I tried not to think of him as a dangerous man I was longing to kiss, but focus instead on the individual parts of his body, muscles, the tendons, the ligaments. I tried to see him only as a patient.

Yes. A patient. Just a body, like a machine. Tissues connected to ligaments connected to muscles. Cells.

Not an amazing masculine body, rippled with muscles and power, attached to the soul of the man who'd teased and challenged me for the past seven-and-a-half weeks as I lived in his castle. The man I thought of before I slept, aware of his bedroom down the hall from mine.

As I ran my hands down the trapezius muscles of his upper back, I tried to calm the rapid beat of my heart. I looked across the room, past all the shiny, modern exercise equipment and weights and yoga mats. Outside the windows, the noon-day sun was peeking through the clouds, a soft pink through the bare black trees, leaving patterns and shadows across the winter-bare garden.

But as I stroked and rubbed Edward beneath my palms, I felt hot as summer. I closed my eyes, trying *not* to imagine what it would be like if he were my lover. How it would feel to sink into the pleasure I imagined he'd give me. Afterward my soul might be ash, but I'd finally know the exhilaration of the fire.

For all these years, I'd guarded both my body and my heart, afraid of ever again feeling the pain of losing someone or something I cared about. But it turned out I hadn't really managed to shield myself from pain. Could anyone?

Sadness and ash came into life anyway. People died. People broke your heart.

Edward sighed. "That feels great."

"I'm glad," I said hoarsely. Dripping more richly scented oil onto his skin, I rubbed the length of his back in silence, the long muscles of his legs, one at a time, to the soles of his feet. Then I lifted the towel a few inches above his body. "Roll over."

He didn't move. "It's, um, not necessary."

"Of course it is." It was difficult to stand there holding the towel away from his naked backside and not look. My tone was waspish. "I have to do your other side. Do you want your muscles to be lopsided? Your back relaxed, your front all stiff?"

"Um…"

"For heaven's sake, just turn over!"

So he did. Exhaling with relief, I gingerly tossed the towel over his front for modesty.

And I saw that his front side was, indeed, stiff. My eyes went wide.

Oh my God, was that—him?

I'd never seen any man naked before. I wasn't seeing him naked now, just the shape of him jutting from his body, almost pornographically explicit beneath the white terry cloth towel, cylindrical and huge. Were all men that large? My cheeks burned, but I stared down at him, fascinated, unable to look away.

Then I felt Edward's gaze. "I took you for a virgin, but you truly don't have any experience at all, do you?"

"I've had lots," I lied. Our eyes met, and my shoulders sagged. "If you mean work. With men—none."

"Not even with Jason?" he said incredulously. "No experience with sex, of any kind?"

The burn of my cheeks had turned radioactive now, and I couldn't meet his gaze. "I've been kissed once or twice."

"You're twenty-eight!"

"I know," I snapped. To hide my embarrassment, I turned away to grab the oil. He'd had a purely physical reaction, I told myself, the automatic response of his hungry male body to the touch of any female. It wasn't that he wanted *me*. Not in particular. It couldn't be.

Could it?

I did a quick comparison between his perfectly chiseled body, his power and wealth and his incredible masculine good looks—and what I had on offer.

Nope.

If you lose an inch of moral high ground, rush back to it as quick as you can, Mrs. Warreldy-

Gribbley advised. Clearing my throat, I said reproachfully. "Keep this professional, please."

"You first," he said, sounding amused. Leaning his head back against his palms, he closed his eyes, and I remembered how he'd caught me staring.

Feeling foolish, I tentatively massaged the muscles of his chest, his arms, his shoulders. I was gentle with the injuries that still hadn't completely healed, but even those were starting to disappear. He was no longer wearing bandages of any kind. There was nothing to keep my hands off his skin as I traced over the twisted muscles, the jagged scars. He was powerful, virile, sexy. He'd nearly vanquished the accident that had devastated his body. Heaven only knew what gaping wound still remained in his heart.

I looked down at him on the massage table. His eyes were still closed, but there was a twist to his lips I couldn't read.

"What are you thinking?" I blurted out. I bit my lip, but there was no taking it back.

His dark blue eyes slit open infinitesimally.

"A dangerous question," he murmured. "Better perhaps for you not to know."

Was he thinking about the accident? The

woman? Or something else entirely? "That's silly." I gave a stilted laugh. "Knowledge is never bad."

"In that case…" His lips curved sardonically. "I am thinking, Miss Maywood, that it would be amusing to seduce you."

A shiver ripped through my body. Wide-eyed, I stepped back from the massage table. "I work for you."

"So?"

"I'm—in love with someone else," I said weakly.

He abruptly sat up. "Not that it matters, but…" He lifted a dark eyebrow. "Are you sure?"

I stared at him. "Of course I'm sure."

"You saw their picture, two movie stars gleaming together on the red carpet, entwined, stupid with love. He cheated on you, left you months ago, you never even slept together—but after all this time, you still love him? You're still faithful? Why?"

Yes, why? My body echoed. Swallowing, I looked at the floor. "I don't know."

"It's true what they say," he said harshly. "The best way to get over someone is to get *under* someone else."

"Really?" I looked at him steadily. "And have

all the women you've slept with burned the image of *her* from your brain—the woman you loved? The woman you almost died for?"

His lips curled, and a low growl came from the back of his throat. "Don't."

"Love doesn't just disappear. You know that as well I do."

"It can. It has. And you're stupid to let it do otherwise." Holding the towel around his hips with one hand, he rose to his feet. His eyes narrowed as he went on the attack. "How does it feel, knowing that your stepsister has everything—the career you want, the man you love?" He tilted his head. "And he probably wanted her from the beginning. He was likely using you, to get to her...."

"Shut up!"

"I feel sorry for you. How it must hurt to know they'll never be punished for hurting you. That while you suffer, they're making love in oblivious joy." He snorted, his lip curling. "You're so meaningless, they've forgotten you even exist."

His face was close to mine, his expression cruel. My heart pounded with grief and pain. Then looking at him, I suddenly understood.

"You're not talking about me," I breathed. "You're talking about yourself."

The air between us was suddenly cold in a way that had nothing to do with the wintery bluster rattling the leaded windows, and the weak afternoon sun falling behind the bare black trees. His lip curled. He turned away.

"We're done."

"No." Reckless of the danger, I grabbed his arm. "I'm trying to make you better," I said in a small voice. "How can I, if I don't understand the depths of your injury?"

Edward looked at me, his jaw tight. "You can see it. You've touched it with your hands."

"Some wounds can't be seen or touched," I whispered. I took a deep breath. "Some go deeper. Let me help you, Edward," I said pleadingly. "Tell me what you need."

His dark blue eyes stared down at me, haunted. Then they turned cold and cruel as the Arctic. Still holding the towel loosely over his hips with one hand, he wrapped the other around the back of my head.

"Here's how you can help me," he said huskily. "Here's what I need."

And he pulled me against him in a hard, hungry kiss.

I didn't have time to resist, or think; my body

tightened, then melted against his. Edward's lips were like silk, hot and fiery with need, his tongue brushing against mine. He held me against him, towering over me, strong and powerful and nearly naked.

Then his towel fell to the floor, and there was no *nearly* about it.

I was wearing a zip-up cotton hoodie, a T-shirt and knit workout pants, as always. But his skin scorched right through my clothes.

His hand moved slowly down my back, as the other cradled the back of my head, his fingers moving through my hair. I felt a whoosh and realized he'd pulled out my ponytail. My hair tumbled down my shoulders. He murmured words against my lips, his voice low, almost a growl.

"I want you, Diana," he breathed, and claimed my lips savagely.

I'd never been kissed like this before. The pallid, tentative kisses of a brief college boyfriend had left me cold. Jason's kisses, as I said, were pleasant, nothing more. This?

This was like fire.

Edward St. Cyr wanted my body. Not my soul. Not my heart. There was no respect in his embrace, no concern for my feelings. There was no emotion at all—just physical need and reckless desire.

But my hunger matched his. He made me forget everything—the past, my broken heart, my pain. When he kissed me, I almost forgot my name. He brought me to life, like a single hot ember from cold ash. He made my body blaze like the sun.

I gripped his bare shoulders with an answering fervor that belonged to some other bolder woman—someone fearless—and kissed him back. With everything I had.

I heard his low hiss of breath, then a rising growl at the back of his throat as he pulled me tighter against his naked body. His hands ran over me possessively. He kissed my lips hard enough to bruise, then nibbled my lower lip. He flicked his hot tongue in each corner of my mouth before he slowly moved down, kissing my chin. Kissing my neck.

My head fell back, my hair tumbling down my shoulders. The cottage seemed to spin around me, as if I were at the center of a tornado. My skin felt hot, burning like the desert. I squeezed my eyes shut. I couldn't open my eyes. If I did, I'd see Edward St. Cyr—my handsome, arrogant boss—kissing down my neck to my chest. If I saw that, I was afraid my mind would explode—along with my body....

His hands brushed roughly over my breasts, over hard, aching nipples. He cupped them over my thin cotton shirt and bra, stroking the sensitive tips with his fingers. My breathing became ragged.

"Take it off," he murmured in my ear, and I felt the flick of his tongue against my ear. Prickles of desire, flashing cold then hot, raced up and down my body. Leaning forward to kiss me, he whispered, "Take it all off."

His hands were insistent against my naked belly as he reached beneath my T-shirt. He reached higher still, toward my thin cotton bra that barely seemed to contain my breasts, which felt strangely tight and heavy, heaving with every gasp of breath. He kissed my lips hard, filling my mouth with his tongue, as he reached to take a breast in his hand. He squeezed an aching nipple.

Sensation ripped through me, and I gasped, gripping his bare shoulders. Electricity coursed through my veins, and blind raging need that frightened me with its intensity.

"I'll help you," he whispered, and pulling on

my sweatshirt, he started to push me down, back onto the massage table.

Abruptly, my eyes flew open.

I realized he intended to take me right here. In the gardener's cottage, surrounded by gym equipment and free weights. Against the massage table. He would ruthlessly help himself to my virginity without any more thought than that he had a hard-on, and I was conveniently available to slake it.

He didn't want *me*. He wanted a *woman*. He intended to make use of me, in the same way I'd scarfed a bag of chips, the times I'd come home from work too starving to wait for a proper meal.

When Edward had kissed me so passionately, when I'd felt his naked body hard and powerful against mine, I'd been overwhelmed with the intensity of sensation. I'd been lost in fantasy and need.

In another moment, I would have let him rip off all my clothes, or—if that was too much trouble—simply pull down my stretchy yoga pants and thrust inside me, like an animal grunting as he took his pleasure, until he left me thirty seconds later, sticky and used upon the table.

None of my romantic dreams had fantasized about *that*.

I pushed on his shoulders. "No."

Edward's heavy-lidded gaze suddenly looked confused. "What?"

My hands pressed harder against his shoulders. I stared up at him in the gray, slanted winter sunlight gleaming dully from the window. Outside, I heard the howl of the wind, the roar of the sea. The barking of a dog. I heard my own thin voice. "I said no."

Looking bewildered, Edward released me, and we stood facing each other beside the table, my clothes disheveled, his entirely absent. I tried not to look down. Tried not to think about how I'd just nearly given him everything—my hungry body and bruised heart—for the sake of blind passion.

But oh, that passion…my body was still trembling with the pleasure of it, with the desperate need. My body hated me right now for stopping. I wanted him still, desperately.

But he had to want me.

Me, Diana, not just any random woman.

All right, so I wasn't exactly a beautiful movie star like Madison. That didn't mean I had to settle for being a stale bag of chips. Not to anyone.

Pulling away, I fisted my hands at my sides.

"You are my patient. There are some lines I will never cross."

"Oh, for…" He gave a low curse. "Surely you've crossed lines before."

I shook my head stubbornly.

"Never broken a single rule?"

"No."

Reaching out, he brushed tendrils of hair from my face, tracing his fingertips down my temple, to my cheek, to my trembling lips. "Then," he whispered, "you've missed a lot of fun."

He towered over me, unselfconscious and proud, though utterly naked. While my own body was trembling. Blood rushed through my veins and I was breathing too fast. I didn't let myself look anywhere but his eyes. Just meeting his hot, hungry gaze was hard enough.

"Let me love you, Diana," he said in a low voice.

For a second, my heart stopped. Then…

"Love me? You said you'll never love anyone."

His breath exhaled on a hiss. "That kind of love is overrated. Hearts and flowers and pledging fidelity forever." His lip curled. "As if you can make emotion permanent by mummifying it in a vow." He took a step closer. "I do like you, Diana. I respect you enough to treat you as my equal—"

"Gee, thanks." My voice was tart.

He placed a finger on my lips. "We both know what is going to happen between us. Pretend otherwise, if you like, but you're fooling no one. Not even yourself." He traced his fingertips along my cheek. "I felt how you just kissed me. You want me, as I want you."

I could hardly deny it. "That doesn't mean I have to act on it."

"Why not?"

I struggled to remember, and finally managed, "Jason—"

"Ah yes. Jason Black, the bright flame in your heart," Edward said mockingly. He shook his head. "Let him keep your heart. I will have your body." He ran his hand gently down my back. "Very soon. And we both know it."

His words shocked me. But I feared he was right. Even now, it was all I could do not to turn my face into his caress.

It would be so easy to surrender. Part of me wanted nothing more than to be bold—to be a rule breaker like he was. What had following the rules ever done for me, except leave me broken-hearted and alone?

If your employer's temptation grows too great,

Mrs. Warreldy-Gribbley had warned, *run as if your life depended on it. It does.*

Trembling, I turned and fled.

"Diana—"

I didn't stop. Tripping over the yoga mat, I wrenched open the door and ran out into the cold garden.

The earlier snowflakes had changed into a chilly, sodden mist that threatened rain. I was nearly crying by the time I made it back to the main house. But the instant I pushed open the heavy oak door, the thick gray walls started to close in on me.

Never broken a single rule?

No.

Then you've missed a lot of fun.

Caesar whined at my feet. Wiping my tears savagely, I looked down to see the sheepdog pacing in front of the door. I'd gotten in the habit of taking him for a walk, since his nominal owner, who was actually and surprisingly Mrs. MacWhirter, had little patience for giving him long walks or letting him sleep on the bed. Getting away suddenly felt absolutely necessary. Grabbing my raincoat and Caesar's leash, I went back out into the rain, the large sheepdog galloping happily beside me.

I walked the opposite direction of the gardener's cottage, heading for the path that led to the rocky edge of the cliffs. The mist had turned to drizzle, already melting down the thin layer of snow, which I knew overnight would harden into ice. Ice like Edward's heart.

Some wounds can't be seen or touched. Some go deeper. Let me help you, Edward. Tell me what you need.

Here's how you can help me. Here's what I need.

Oh. Oh, oh, oh. I abruptly stopped on the path, causing Caesar to jump beside me, before he ran ahead with a snuff.

That was the reason Edward had kissed me. Not because he wanted me. Not even just because he wanted a woman. Oh no.

He'd kissed me to shut me up. Because I'd been asking about his accident, probing with questions he didn't want to answer. He'd deflected me the easiest, simplest way he knew how. The way that always worked with any woman.

My cheeks were burning now, my throat aching with humiliation. Tears streaked down my face, leaving cold trails beneath the chill of the wind, as I looked out at the vast gray sea.

Edward St. Cyr was used to riding roughshod over people, especially women. He was used to twisting them all around his finger. I knew this. And I'd still let him do it to me.

I stared out at the ocean, watching the light's play of sparkle and shadows. My tangled hair flew around me in the chilly wind. Watching the seagulls fly away, I almost wished I could join them. To fly away and disappear and never be seen again.

Penryth Hall was supposed to be my place to hide. How did you hide from a hiding place?

Maybe there was nowhere to hide, I thought suddenly, when the person you were really trying to hide from was yourself.

Sooner or later, I'd have to go back to California. Face the scandal, the pity. Face the two people who'd ripped out my heart. And most of all: face myself.

Picking up a stick, I tossed it down the beach. With an eager yelp, Caesar ran after it. My mouth still felt seared from Edward's kiss. I touched my bruised lips. They still ached for him. For that one single moment, when I'd thought Edward wanted me—me, the invisible girl, completely unnoteworthy either in looks, intelligence or career—I'd felt like I was worth something. Like I *mattered.*

I writhed with shame to remember it now.

Caesar barked happily, dropping the stick at my feet. I picked it up and tossed it farther down the rocky shore. I stayed out there, procrastinating for as long as I could. But by the time we were both wet with rain and freezing cold, I'd made up my mind.

I was leaving Penryth Hall.

As the dog raced ahead on the return path, I realized I'd finally found something that frightened me more than going back to California.

Staying here.

Edward didn't really need me anyway. Not anymore. I'd known that when I'd seen him running on the treadmill today.

"You don't need me," I said aloud.

Need me, need me, the wind sighed mournfully in return.

As Caesar hurried ahead of me on the wet path, his tongue lolling out as he raced eagerly to get back home to the castle of gray stone, my steps became slower. When I finally reached the door, my feet turned to the left, and I found myself walking around the house to the front door, procrastinating the moment I'd have to go inside and tell him I was leaving. Once I said it, I'd have to do it.

I stopped in shock.

Two expensive sedans were parked in front of Penryth Hall. Standing next to them were my stepsister's two bodyguards, Damian and Luis.

I stared at them, goggle-eyed. "What are you…"

"Hello, Diana," Luis said, smiling. "Long time no see."

But next to him, Damian glowered down at me. "Miss Lowe and Mr. Black are here to see you." Seven feet tall, bald, and scowling, he shook his head at me. "And she's really, really mad at you."

CHAPTER THREE

WATER DRIPPED NOISILY from my raincoat to the flagstones as I walked nervously into the shadowy foyer of the castle. The thought of facing them all at once scared me to death.

Edward, Madison and Jason.

All at once.

I couldn't do it. I stopped, clenched my hands at my sides.

Caesar loped up beside me in the foyer. With a sympathetic look, he shook his fur, splattering me with water and mud. I gasped as cold wet dirt hit my face, then gasped again as I looked down at my messed-up hair, my muddy raincoat and sneakers. I hadn't buttoned the raincoat so even the T-shirt beneath, which Edward had recently groped, now had a splatter of mud across the front.

If I thought I couldn't face them before…!

With a satisfied snort, Caesar trotted happily down the hall, no doubt intending to plunk himself in his nice spot on the rug in front of the fire. What did he have to fear? *He* wasn't facing the firing squad.

I heard voices down the hall, coming from the library. Madison's high-pitched voice, two lower masculine ones. Sharing tea, or lying in ambush for me?

Maybe I could make a run for it. If I tiptoed down the hall, I'd sneak by the library unseen. Then I'd pack my bag and flee for Tierra del Fuego.

"What are you doing?" Edward said quietly.

He was standing in the hallway, his face in silhouette. He'd showered and changed from his exercise clothes. His dark hair was still wet, slicked back against his head, and he was actually wearing a jacket and tie, button-up shirt and trousers. It was…sexy. I licked my lips. "Why are you dressed up?"

"We have company." Flickering firelight from the open doorway of the library cast shadows on his grim face. "Care to join us?"

He was so handsome and sophisticated. Everything I was not. It seemed incredible to me now that he'd kissed me, for any reason whatsoever. I put my hand to my hair. Yup. Just as I thought, it was damp with rain, tangled as a bird's nest. I put my hand down.

"Well?"

"I don't think I can do this," I whispered. My heart was pounding, my feet ready to take flight. "I thought about it on my walk. After all that's happened, I've realized you don't need me anymore and maybe it's time for me to just—"

"Is that you, Diana?" Madison's voice carried sharply from the library. "Get in here!"

Edward's eyebrow lifted. He came closer, and I shivered as he pulled my raincoat off my body. I felt the brush of his fingertips. I breathed in his scent, masculine and clean, like a Bavarian forest. Hanging up the wet coat, he turned back to me.

"You're going to have to face them sooner or later, Diana," he said quietly. His hand fell bracingly on my shoulder. "Might as well be now."

His camaraderie made me feel strangely comforted, even strengthened. That brief moment helped me square my shoulders, lift my chin and walk with my head held high into the library.

The firelit room was impossibly elegant, two stories high, with leatherbound books on all sides, a ladder to reach them and an enormous white marble fireplace at one end. Not to mention two movie stars sitting on the white leather sofa near the fire.

Madison looked beautiful as always. Her long blond hair was straight, her eyes huge beneath fake eyelashes, her cheekbones sharp enough to cut glass. Even casually dressed in a white cropped jacket of tousled fur, thousand-dollar silk blouse and size 0 toothpick jeans, no one could have mistaken her for anything but a movie star.

Jason sat beside her, his hand protectively on her knee. Handsome, broad shouldered and corn-fed like the Texas farm boy he'd once been, he looked different than he had just six months ago. The gloss of success covered him now, like his newly expensive clothes.

Looking at them, my body flashed hot, then cold. Jason started to rise to his feet, but Madison grabbed his hand, keeping him seated beside her.

"Diana," she said coolly. "It was rude of you to keep us waiting. But I don't blame you for being afraid to face me after what you did."

I would have staggered back, except Edward was behind me, his hand supportively on my lower back. I felt his strength and somehow my knees steadied themselves.

"What *I* did?" I queried dangerously.

"You left me when I needed you most!"

I gaped at her. "I went to California to give the reporter a tour of your house—as you asked me to!"

She waved her hand dismissively. "That? All that happened ages ago. I'm talking about my movie premiere last night. You should have been there for me!"

"Are you kidding?" I breathed.

"You know how nervous I get, being at public events. You promised you'd always be there...."

"Yeah, when I was your assistant." I swallowed looking between her and Jason. "Before I was completely humiliated in front of the whole world—"

"Are you still trying to punish me for that?" she demanded. "We didn't mean to fall in love. It was an accident. When it's right, you just know." She looked lovingly at Jason, then glared at me. "It's petty of you, Diana, it really is, and I'm disappointed. You and Jason didn't even sleep together."

"You told her that?" I breathed, staring down at him.

Rubbing the back of his blond head, Jason gave

me the rueful smile I used to find so irresistible. "You and I were friends, Diana. We dated and yeah, there was a little flirting going on, but hell," he shook his head, "you never let me touch you. Said you wanted to wait for true love or some such...but this is the twenty-first century. I don't know what century you're living in, but as far as I'm concerned, if there's no sex, there's no relationship."

For a second I couldn't breathe. No relationship? As if I'd imagined it all in my mind? "You—"

And it was then I saw the sparkle on Madison's left hand.

A huge canary-yellow diamond ring.

On *that* finger.

With an intake of breath, I covered my mouth with my hand. For a moment, the only sound in the library was the crackle of the fire in counterpoint to the miserable drip-drip-drip of water from my hair as I stood like a mud-splattered, drowned rat in front of my beautiful stepsister, who had a ten-carat engagement ring on one hand, and the man I'd loved holding the other.

"You're—" I was horrified to feel tears burning the backs of my eyelids as I looked between them. "You're engaged?"

Madison put her hand over the ring. "Yes…" A smile softened the sharp lines of her face as she looked at Jason. "He asked me last night, after the premiere."

Jason smiled back. Lifting her hand to his lips, he kissed it. "Best night of my life."

Their eyes glowed as they looked at each other. They were in love. Really, deeply in love. It was one thing to know it in my mind, and something else entirely to see it right in front of me. I not only felt sick, I felt invisible. An echo went through my mind.

I feel sorry for you. How it must hurt to know they'll never be punished for hurting you. That while you suffer, they're making love in oblivious joy. You're so meaningless, they've forgotten you even exist.

"Stop pouting and be happy for us." Madison turned back to me. "Come back and work for me. I need you. Someone will have to coordinate with the wedding planner…"

Wedding planner!

"And don't worry," Jason said to me kindly. "You'll find a real boyfriend someday, Di. Great girl like you. It's bound to happen, even if it takes a while…"

Violently, I held up a trembling hand, unable to bear another patronizing word. My heart was collapsing in my chest, squeezing into hard little pieces, about to fly out of my ribs like bullets. In another moment, I'd weep in front of them, and then I really would have to die.

"Darling." Edward purred behind me, suddenly wrapping his arms around me. Pulling me back protectively against his body, he murmured, "Didn't you tell them?"

I looked back at him blankly. "Tell them?"

He smiled down at me, his expression tender, his dark blue gaze caressing mine. "About us."

"Us?" I said.

"Us." Edward looked at me as if it were all he could do right now not to lift me up in his arms and carry me upstairs to bed. No man had looked at me like that before. Not ever. The full seductive force of his gaze was a blast of heat, an intoxicating drug that made every part of me yearn to tremble and unfold like a flower. "Diana, why didn't you tell them..." he stroked back a tendril of my hair, "that we're lovers?"

What? My heart stopped beating.

"What?" Madison said.

"What?" Jason said.

Edward looked down at me with concern. "But darling, you're chilled to the bone. Your clothes are wet. Were you taking the dog on a walk?"

Teeth chattering—and not just from cold—I nodded like a fool.

He gave me a slow, sensual smile. "Why don't you go upstairs to our room—" *our* room? I thought dumbly "—and change. We'll wait."

"I will *not* wait," Madison snapped. "Not until you agree to come back and plan our wedding." Looking between Edward and me, no doubt comparing his perfect gorgeousness to my slovenly mess, she added suspiciously, "And I don't believe for a second that the two of you…"

Edward didn't even look her way. "Actually, Diana," he whispered, twining a long muddy, tangled tendril of my hair as if it were silken perfection, "I think I'll come upstairs. Help you out of these cold, wet clothes."

Any woman could get warm instantly, just by looking up into Edward's hot dark gaze. Had I wandered into some strange parallel universe, where I was the beautiful movie star, instead of Madison? Had I fallen on my walk and hit my head on a rock?

I felt my stepsister's gaze travel over us both,

from the way I was standing to the way that Edward supported my arm. There was new doubt in her melodious voice as she said, "You're really—together?"

"Only recently," Edward said, smiling down at me hungrily, cupping my cheek with his hand. As if he were already thinking about what he intended to do to me in bed. "I wanted Diana from the moment we met. But she tortured me," his eyes traced mine, "making me wait. And wait. The sexiest, most desirable woman in the world."

"She's just a physical therapist." Madison sounded grumpy.

Edward finally looked at her. "Yes. A healer. And what Diana knows about the human body—" He exhaled, looking at me in wonder. "No wonder she's the most amazing lover I've ever had."

My body flashed hot, then cold.

"The two of you are in love?" Jason said, dumbfounded.

"Love?" Edward snorted. "No." He looked down at me, stroking my cheek, and I felt his fingertips against my skin. "What we have is purely physical. Sex. And fire."

A little sound came from the back of Jason's

throat as he stared between us, his eyes comically huge.

"I don't understand." Madison's beautiful face was bewildered, as if she was confused how any other woman could be the center of a man's attention when she herself was in the room. "It's only been a couple months."

"When it's right, you just know." He smiled as he echoed her earlier words. Wrapping both his strong arms around me, he pulled me back against his chest. "I'm sorry Diana's not available to be your assistant, Madison. But after your long trip from London, perhaps the two of you will join us for dinner?"

"Uh." Jason couldn't stop staring at me, as if he'd never quite seen me before. "I don't think…"

"Of course we will." Madison looked at Edward with new, almost proprietary interest. "I look forward to getting to know your new boyfriend, Diana."

"Good," Edward replied, as if he hadn't noticed her sudden pointed look, like a cat who'd just noticed a particularly appealing mouse. But I'd noticed it. And by the crease in his forehead, so had Jason. "Please excuse us while I take Diana upstairs." His voice lingered wickedly on the word *take.* "In the meantime help yourselves to tea, or there's drinks at the bar if you'd like something stronger."

Edward pulled me out into the hall.

"*I* need something stronger," I muttered.

"Hsst," he said beneath his breath. Holding my hand, he drew me down the echoing flagstones of the dark hallway and up the sweeping stairs. It wasn't until we were at my bedroom door that I stopped, looking at him with my brow creased.

"You made them think we were lovers."

"Yes."

"Why?"

"Because I felt like it."

I swallowed, shaking my head. "I don't under-stand."

Edward's eyes narrowed. "They were treating you so badly. Trying to guilt you into *planning their wedding. Don't worry, you'll find a real boyfriend someday,*" he mimicked Jason, then snorted with a flare of nostril. "Supercilious, con-descending prats."

An unwilling laugh burbled to my lips, then faded. "But maybe they were right," I said softly, looking down. "I should have known he'd choose

Madison over me. And I don't have a boyfriend. I'm starting to think I'll never—"

"Don't be an idiot." He put his hand against my cheek. "You could have any man you want, any time you want. If you don't have one at the moment, it's by your choice."

I swallowed, looking up at him. "You're being very kind, but…"

"I'm not kind." He paused. "I just didn't like them treating you as if you were invisible. As if you were nobody."

"I am nobody," I whispered.

Dropping his hand, he gave a low heartfelt curse. "For the last two months, you've matched me toe-to-toe, like a fighter. An equal. But the instant you walked into the library, you changed into a timid little mouse. What happened?"

"Why do you care?" I forced myself to meet his eyes. "You were *running* on the treadmill today, Edward. You don't even need a physical therapist anymore." I shook my head a little tearfully. "It's time for me to—"

"Oh, no, you don't," he said furiously. "Don't even *think* about using that as an excuse to run away. Why do I care? Because I don't like to see the woman who regularly brings me to my knees—that's you—falling apart at the feet of those vapid, self-absorbed idiots!"

"When did I bring you to your knees?" I said stupidly.

He looked down at me. "Have you already forgotten," he said softly, "how just two hours ago, I took you in my arms and begged you to make love to me? I was putty in your hands."

A shiver went over me, starting from my tingling, bruised lips. Tossing my head, I tried to laugh. "I don't remember any begging—"

My sentence cut off as he pulled me abruptly into his arms. His fingertips stroked down my cheek, skimming lightly down my jaw, my neck. I trembled beneath his touch, feeling the warm caress of his breath, the heat of his powerful body against mine.

"This is how I beg," he whispered, his lips close to mine, making me burn, making me lose my breath. Slowly, he kissed me, softly, so softly. "You're strong, Diana. And brave." His lips flickered like a whisper of breath against mine. "Why are you suddenly pretending not to be?" He moved back, and his expression changed, almost to a glare. "I want the woman I hired, the one who's constantly trying to kick my ass. Bring her back."

I licked my lips. "It's hard…"

"No. It's easy. Be your real self again, or get the hell out of my house."

My lips parted in shock. It was funny. I'd been planning to leave Penryth Hall, talking myself into it. But the thought of Edward kicking me out suddenly felt unbearable.

"You're firing me?" I said faintly. The way he looked at me made me shiver. My heart pounded, and my lips tingled in memory. "You don't understand. Madison and I have a history. And Jason—" My voice stopped.

"You still love him?" His eyes grew hard. "You're a fool. But that's what love does," he said grimly. "Makes us fools."

Thinking of Jason, sitting next to Madison on the couch as he said patronizingly, *If there's no sex, there's no relationship,* I shook my head. "I don't know what I feel anymore."

"Whatever. Doesn't matter. Pull yourself together. You're better than this, Diana. And I'm not interested in watching you let them wipe their feet on you." He glared at me. "Either stop acting like a doormat or you can ask them for a ride back to London."

I stared up at him, feeling faint, assaulted on all sides. How I wished I could be the woman he described—the one who was brave and strong. But the thought of facing them and telling them what I really thought.... Jason...and Madison...

"I don't think I can do it," I choked out.

"You have twenty minutes to decide." Edward's jaw tightened. Turning away, he stopped at the bedroom door. "Take a shower. Brush your hair. Get on dry clothes. When you come back downstairs for dinner, I'll see your answer."

My legs were shaking as I came downstairs a half hour later. I'd taken my time in the shower, closing my eyes beneath the hot steam. I combed out my wet hair, then started to reach in the closet for my typical wardrobe of casual T-shirt and cargo pants. Then I stopped.

Instead, I took out a skirt and blouse, and black high-heeled shoes. I put on red lipstick, which I'd almost forgotten I owned, and a headband. Then I looked at myself in the mirror. It looked like me, but not me. It looked like the me that I used to be, in high school. Before Mom had gotten sick. Before Madison had taken the dream I'd wanted.

You're strong, Diana. And brave. Why are you suddenly pretending not to be?

As I came downstairs, I could hear that the three of them had already started dinner without me in the medieval great hall. Well, Edward had told me twenty minutes. He was probably starting to wonder if I'd decided to pack for London.

I was still wondering myself.

I could play it safe, say nothing tonight and quietly leave with Madison, back to my old life. I could plan their wedding, be silently helpful and invisible.

Or—

Or I could be brave enough to be myself. And tell Jason and Madison how I really felt. Then I could remain at Penryth Hall—but I'd almost certainly end up in Edward's bed.

Let him keep your heart. I will have your body. Very soon. And we both know it.

Yes. I swallowed. If I stayed here, it would happen. Sooner or later. Probably sooner. I wouldn't be able to resist for much longer. I'd give my virginity to a playboy who wanted only a physical affair. It would be just sex, as he'd said.

Sex. And fire.

I felt dizzy just thinking of it.

So which would it be?

Remain invisible, mute and untouched?

Or risk everything, be honest and brave—but know that it would irrevocably change my life?

Standing outside the great hall, I still didn't know. I was caught between longing and fear. But I was already late. Clutching my hands into fists, I took a deep breath and walked in.

Madison had appropriated the place of honor at the long, candlelit dining table, with Jason on her right side and Edward on her left. Edward saw me, and his expression sharpened.

"You're here," he said, motioning toward the place to his left. Avoiding his gaze, I slid quietly into the chair beside him at the table.

Glancing at me dismissively, my stepsister didn't break stride in her story, which was mostly explaining the unbearable burdens of being young, rich, famous and beautiful. "You'd think I'd be used to press junkets by now," she finished with a sigh, moving her hands gracefully over the long, gleaming table, to make her enormous diamond ring sparkle in the candlelight. "But the one this morning was especially exhausting. They barely let me plug the movie. They just wanted to know about our engagement." She gave Jason a flirtatious sideways glance. "They wanted every detail. How he proposed, when the wedding will be…" Madison turned to me. "Why did you take so long, Diana? We're halfway through our dinner."

It was worth it, to miss most of your story, I thought. But I didn't have the nerve to say it.

"Sorry," I mumbled, and reaching for the silver tray at the center of the table, I pulled off the lid and served myself some rosemary lamb, herbed red potatoes and vegetables. Then I saw the basket, and gave a happy smile. "Mrs. MacWhirter made fresh rolls!"

"I asked her to, this morning," Edward said, smiling back. "I know they're your favorite."

"Bread makes you fat, you know," Madison said.

But skipping bread makes you mean, I thought. I said only, "Aren't Damian and Luis joining us?"

"They're eating in the kitchen with the staff."

"Smart," I mumbled.

"What?" Madison said.

"Nothing." I sighed. I felt Edward tighten up beside me. I could almost feel his glower.

I tried to eat, but sitting with Madison and

Edward I could barely taste the food. Even the freshly baked white bun tasted ashy.

"Anyway," Madison continued, "sometimes I just get tired of all the attention." She yawned in a showy way, stretching her hands upward, showing off her figure to clear advantage. Then she flashed her beguiling smile, her trademark that no man could resist, first at Jason, then—at Edward. "Our engagement is news all over the world. My fans everywhere are thrilled... They're so sweet, sending congratulations and gifts." She gave a tinkly laugh that sounded like music. "Though I've had a few male fans threaten to throw themselves out windows unless I cancel the wedding. You know how it is, I'm sure." Reaching out, she patted Edward's hand. "How difficult it is, when people want you constantly."

My eyes went wide as I stared at Madison's perfectly manicured hand. Patting over Edward's. Slowly. Languorously. Like a dance.

Pat, pat, pat.

With the same hand that held the ten-carat diamond engagement ring given to her by another man.

She wanted Edward's attention now, too, I realized. Why was I surprised? It had happened all our lives. Madison always had to be the center of male approval. Even when we were teenagers, and my mother was dying, Madison had snuck away with the pool cleaner and smashed her father's car into a palm tree—effectively pulling Howard's attention away from my mom.

All our lives, I'd tried to look out for Madison. I'd tried to treat her like the sister I'd always wanted, back when I was a lonely only child. But she'd just taken from me, and taken more.

But as I watched her hand with the huge diamond ring pat Edward's on the table—*pat, pat, pat*—I suddenly couldn't stand it one second more.

"Are you seriously flirting with Edward now?" I said incredulously. "What the hell is *wrong* with you, Madison?"

She stared at me, her gorgeous pink mouth a round O. Then she ripped her hand off Edward's as if it had burned her. "I wasn't flirting with him! I'm an engaged woman!" She glared at me, then turned to give her fiancé a tender glance. "I'm in love with Jason."

"Are you? Are you really? Do you even know what it means?"

"Of course I do—we're engaged!"

"So what? You've been engaged five times!"

"Really?" Edward said, looking at me with growing joy.

"Five?" Jason gasped.

"You're crazy!" she said in outrage. Then, as the two men stared at her, she moderated her expression and said more calmly, "I haven't been engaged five times."

"No? Let's see." I tilted my head thoughtfully. "That punk rock musician you met on Hollywood Boulevard..."

"You call *that* an engagement?" Glancing at Jason and Edward, she trilled a little laugh. "I was fifteen! It lasted six days!"

"But Rhiannon never talked to you again."

Madison tossed her head. "He loved me, not her. She should have accepted that."

"Yes. He loved you. For six days, till his band left for Las Vegas. For that, you destroyed a friendship you'd had since kindergarten." I lifted an eyebrow and inquired coolly, "How many friends do you have left now, by the way, Maddy?"

She looked at me in wide-eyed fury. "I have plenty of friends, believe me!"

"*Friends.* People who suck up to you," I murmured. "People who need something from you.

People who laugh at your jokes even when they're not funny. Are those really friends? Or are they employees?"

"Shut up!"

Picking up my fork, I idly traced it along my plate, crushing my potatoes against the gold-rimmed china, creating a pattern like tracks through snow. "Then when you were sixteen, there was the man who cleaned our pools..."

"A pool cleaner? That wasn't an engagement, it was a cry for help!"

"Right." I gave her a tight smile. "You were trying to get Howard's attention. He'd been neglecting you, spending so much time at my mom's deathbed. Drove you crazy."

She tossed me an irritated, petulant glance. "You make me sound selfish, but for months and months it dragged on. A girl needs her father!"

The casual cruelty of her words took my breath away. *For months and months it dragged on.* Yes. It had taken my mom months and months to die. Months of her fighting her illness with courage, long after hope was gone. Months of her fading away, so sweet and brave, still trying so hard to take care of everyone, even Madison. My jaw hardened.

"I know. I was there. Every day. All day." I ticked off another finger in a violent gesture. "Third engagement. My agent."

"*Your* agent?" Edward said in surprise.

"Yeah." I looked at him. "We met at Howard's wrap party for a film. Lenny signed me when I was almost seventeen. I worked on a soap opera for about six months before Mom got sick."

"You were on a television show?" he said incredulously.

"I quit to stay home with her." And I'd quit without regret. I'd missed my friends, and the tutor was a poor replacement for school. I'd felt lonely. "I didn't try to act again until months later, when my agent sent me a script. He wanted to pitch me as a 'fresh new face' to star in a Disney show for preteens. My mom convinced me to go to the audition. But on my way there, I got a message from Howard that Mom had just had a seizure. He wasn't sure she'd make it…." My lips quivered at the edges. "She did. That time. But when I went back to do the audition two days later, the part was gone. The show had already hired someone else." I turned to look at Madison. "*Moxie McSocksie* made you a star."

Edward frowned. "*Moxie* what?"

"I'm surprised you haven't heard of it." I turned to him wearily. "Moxie. You know. Regular student by day, adventurous cub reporter by night. It was a huge hit."

"*Moxie Mc*—" Frowning, he looked at Madison, his eyes wide. "I remember. Your face was on the side of buses for months when the show came to London. It was your big break, wasn't it? Made you famous. Made you rich."

Wide-eyed, Madison looked from Edward, to Jason, to me. She abruptly slapped her hands hard against the table.

"I deserved the role, not you!" she cried in a shrill voice. "I'd been doing commercials since I was a baby! I was the actress, not you. And you were eighteen by then, Diana, way too old for the role!"

"Compared to you?"

"I was seventeen—the perfect age!"

"For getting engaged to my agent?" I said dryly. "The second you heard about the role, you went for him. You knew he could get you that audition, and more. He could get you the career you wanted."

"You make it sound sordid," she gasped, putting her manicured hand against her chest in a fake laugh. "It wasn't like that!"

"Oh?" I said coolly. "So you didn't seduce him to get him to take you on as a client, and sell you to the show?"

"You're jealous! It's not my fault you gave up the audition and rushed home. The next day, when Lenny and I spent time together, he realized I was the perfect Moxie, not you. That's all!"

"He was fifty," I said.

"I loved him!"

"You dumped him fast enough, after he got you your first movie role, and you realized that dating a big Hollywood director would help you further up the ladder. You didn't mind that he had to break up with his *wife* to do it."

"Enough." Jason rose from the table, his face like granite. He looked at Madison. "So I'm number five, am I?"

"You're different," she whispered. "Special."

"I don't feel special." Jason looked at me. "I'm starting to think I chose the wrong sister."

Madison looked frightened. "Jason—"

"Here." Reaching into his pocket, he tossed a set of car keys onto the table. They skittered helter-skelter down the long polished wood. "I'm taking a car back to London. I'll leave the keys at the front desk of your hotel."

"Wait," she said desperately, rising to her feet. "You can't leave. I need you—"

He left without a backward glance.

Madison staggered back.

"Does this mean the wedding is off?" Edward inquired pleasantly.

Ignoring him, she slowly turned to face me. "Diana. I know I've done a lot of stupid and self-ish things. But I never thought you would be the one to list them out. Not you."

The injured fury in my heart deserted me, just when I needed it most. I rose to my feet.

"I never thought you would attack me like that." Her crystalline eyes glimmered in the candlelight. Her voice caught as she looked away. "You're not my big sister. You're just like all the rest."

My throat suddenly hurt as I remembered how we first met, virtual strangers to each other attending our parents' wedding as slightly-too-old flower girls, both feeling awkward, uncertain. My mom had told me Madison's mother died of a drug overdose when she was a toddler. *So be nice to her*, she'd chided.

Seeing her sad little face, I'd wanted to protect

her. *We're family now,* I'd said at the wedding, hugging her over the flowers. *I'm gonna be your big sister, Maddy. So don't worry. I'll take care of you.*

"Maddy—" I whispered.

"Forget it," Madison choked out. "Just forget it."

She turned away in a cloud of grief and expensive perfume, stumbling out of Penryth Hall, calling Jason's name, then her bodyguards'.

The great hall was suddenly quiet, the only sound the whipping of the wind outside rattling the glass panes of the windows.

Edward looked at me.

"I wondered what it would be like, if you ever really let yourself go," he said quietly. "Now I know."

A sob lifted to my throat. My knees wobbled beneath me, and suddenly Edward was there, catching me before I could fall. I stared up at him in bewilderment, wondering how he'd moved so fast.

"I was horrible," I whispered.

"You were magnificent," he said softly, brushing hair from my face.

"Magnificent?" I gave a harsh laugh. "I was

so determined to list all her faults. But what I've done is worse."

"What's that?"

"I told her I'd always take care of her," I whispered. "Then I hurt her like this…."

"Seems like she had it coming," he said softly, caressing my cheek.

I shuddered at his touch, longing for his comfort, fighting the desire to turn my cheek into his caress. "All these years I've blamed her for taking the role that might have made me a star. But it was never mine in the first place. She was right. I had the chance to audition. I went home."

"To be with your mother…"

"Whatever the reason. It was a choice I made." I wiped my eyes with the back of my hand. "After losing my parents, and the role of Moxie, I never wanted to have my heart crushed again. It's not Madison's fault I spent the next ten years hiding, not letting myself feel or want too much…."

"Until you fell for Jason," he said.

But was Jason the exception? Or had he just been one more example of me taking the safe path? The thought was new and troubling.

Swallowing, I looked up at Edward through shimmering tears.

"It wasn't Madison's fault," I whispered. "I did it to myself. I chose to be a coward." My voice caught as I turned away. "Playing it safe has ruined my life."

Edward said quietly, "Your life isn't over yet."

Our eyes locked in the shadowy great hall. An almost palpable electricity crackled between us.

"I have a private island in the Caribbean," he said huskily. "That's where I'd go if I needed to escape a broken heart. I stayed there after my accident. I needed to be alone." He gave a grim smile. "Well, alone with a doctor and two round-the-clock nurses." Reaching out, he gently twisted a long tendril of my hair. "No one can get at you there, Diana. There's no internet, no phones, no way to even get on the island except by my plane." He gave me a smile. "Want to go?"

Looking up at him, I tried to smile back, but couldn't quite manage. "Thanks, but it wouldn't help." I looked down at my hands. "Not when the person I want to escape from is myself."

Reaching out, Edward tilted up my chin, forcing me to meet his gaze. His dark blue eyes gleamed with silver and sapphire light, like the half-bright sky at dawn. "I understand," he said quietly. "Better than you might think."

"You do?" I whispered. Of its own will, my hand reached up to stroke his tousled black hair. It was so thick, and soft, just as I'd thought it would be. Five o'clock shadow traced the sharp edges of his jaw. Everything about him was masculine and foreign to me. I didn't understand him at all. "Why are you being so nice to me?"

He gave a sudden crooked smile. "Maybe it's just to lure you in my bed." His hand moved gently from my hair to my cheek. "Did you ever think of that?"

I gave a tearful, hiccupping laugh. "You don't have to try this hard for me."

"I don't?"

I looked up at him.

"No," I whispered.

His hand froze on my cheek. His expression changed as he looked down at me.

Cupping my face in his large, strong hands, Edward lowered his mouth to mine, slowly, deliberately. I could have pulled back from his embrace at any time. But I didn't move. I held my breath in anticipation as time suspended.

Then his lips finally touched mine, and I exhaled with a sigh. My breath comingled and joined with his. His lips were tantalizingly soft at first, sweet and warm. He lured me in, made me lean forward against his chest, reaching up to wrap my arms around his shoulders. Then he shifted me in his grip. As he held me more tightly, the world started to whirl around us.

He'd seen me at my worst, but he still wanted me....

His kiss deepened, became hungrier, more demanding. I clutched his hard, powerful body to my own, like a woman seeking shelter in a storm. Edward was solid, like a fortress in my arms. And if somewhere in the back of my mind, a voice shouted at me to stop, telling me this would destroy me, I pushed it away. I clutched Edward to me, kissing him with every cell in my body, my skin hot with need.

I was tired of being safe.

With a low growl, Edward lifted me up into his arms. Leaving the great hall, he carried me up the sweeping stairs.

Held against his chest, I looked up at him, dazed, lost in desire. I watched the play of shadows against his hard, handsome face as he carried me up the stairs. He carried my weight like a feather.

Edward St. Cyr was taking me to his bed. In

just moments, my virginity would irrevocably be taken by this cold playboy, this breaker of hearts.

But he was so much more than that.

Lifting my hand to his cheek in wonder, I felt the roughness of his skin, the dark bristles along the hard edge of his jaw. He was so powerful. So masculine. So different from me in every way.

And yet somehow, tonight, I felt we were not so different. Out of anyone on earth, Edward understood me. He'd seen the scared girl I'd been, and the bold woman I wanted to be. He knew me....

Using his shoulder, Edward pushed open his bedroom door. I'd never been inside it before. The room was dark with shadows. Dark, Spartan furniture lined the edges of the walls.

A large white bed was at the center of the black-lacquered floor, illuminated by a pool of moonlight from the window like a spotlight.

Kicking the door closed behind us, Edward gently set me down on the moonswept, king-size bed. He hadn't said a word since we'd left the great hall. I looked up at him, shivering in my headband and simple skirt and blouse. I was twenty-eight years old, but felt as innocent as a schoolgirl.

Never taking his eyes off me, Edward slowly

pulled off his tie. He dropped it to the lacquered floor. He moved toward the bed.

And I started to shake.

Moonlight glazed the bed around me as his strong hands tangled in my hair. "This is the first thing to go," he murmured, and he pulled my headband aside. Bracing his arms on the mattress around me, he leaned forward. Gently, he kissed me. His mouth seared mine, pushing my lips apart as he pushed me back against the bed.

My head fell back against the soft pillows, and he gave my cheeks little feather-soft kisses before returning to my mouth. His tongue flicked possessively between my lips before he trailed kisses down my throat. My head tilted back as I gave a soft gasp. Feeling lost. Feeling new.

"I don't love you," I breathed—speaking to him? Or myself?

"No." His dark blue eyes gleamed. "You want me. Say it."

My voice was almost too quiet to hear. "I want you."

"Louder."

I lifted my gaze. "I want you."

My voice had turned strong. Dangerous. Reckless.

He looked at me with such intensity I forgot to breathe.

"And I want you."

Lowering his mouth hard against my own, Edward pushed me deeper into the soft white pillows. His hands stroked slowly down my body, light as a whisper, hot as a desert wind. His kiss deepened. Reaching down, he cupped my breasts that were aching beneath my prim white shirt.

I barely felt his fingertips move against my blouse. The buttons were just suddenly undone, and the unwilling thought crossed my mind that he'd had a lot of experience. He pulled my body up, and my blouse vanished into thin air, revealing my flimsy bra of blue silk.

What had made me wear my only truly pretty bra today, underneath my blouse? A coincidence? Or had I known, even before I came downstairs for dinner, that I intended to end my night this way?

"So beautiful," he whispered, his hands touching everywhere, sliding over my bare skin. "You've been driving me mad…."

"Me too…" I breathed. We'd been both alone, I realized, both wounded deep inside, in injuries we'd caused ourselves. But in this moment, it felt like loneliness no longer existed. My heart and my arms were both overflowing. We were together. We were the same....

I pulled him down hard against my body, wanting to feel his weight over mine. I heard the appreciative murmur from the back of his throat as I kissed him, hard, and tried to unbutton his shirt. My hands were trembling and clumsy.

"Stop," he said huskily, putting his hands over mine. For a moment, I was afraid he'd changed his mind. Then I realized he was unbuttoning his shirt for me, his expert fingers doing it three times as fast. Rising from the bed, he unbuttoned his cuffs and dropped his expensive tailored shirt to the dark floor. I gasped when I saw the muscles and planes of his naked chest, lit by the slanted moonlight. I'd seen his body before, during massage and occasionally when I'd taken him to swim at the local center. But never like this. Never with the full knowledge that I could run my hands over his skin, that I'd soon feel his naked body roughly take my own.

Edward's eyes never left mine as he deliberately undid his trousers and pulled them with his silk boxers down his thickly chiseled thighs. A choked noise came from the back of my throat as he stood naked in front of me. He'd been naked in the gym that morning, but I'd been afraid to look. I was still a little afraid now. Blushing, I started to look away.

His gaze locked with mine, challenging me. With a deep breath, I lifted my chin, and looked, really looked, at his naked body.

He was not ashamed, standing there with quiet pride and giving me time to look, to accept. His shoulders were broad, and a dusting of dark hair trailed like a V from his nipples and hard-muscled chest down to a taut, flat waist. His legs were powerful as a warrior's, and as he shifted his weight in front of me, he moved with an athlete's grace. His thighs were hard and huge. Which could also describe what I saw if I dared to look between his thighs… But there my nerve failed me.

He was powerful. He'd been healed. But the injuries had left scars that couldn't be denied. The raised scars across his torso, where his ribs had been broken, left white lines across perfect olive-toned skin. Similar lines slashed brutally across his right shoulder and arm, and his left leg, like cobwebs of his body's memory, forgiven but not forgotten.

Men prey on the tender weakness of the feminine heart, Mrs. Warreldy-Gribbley had warned. *He will lure you into bed by using your own heart against you.*

Turning away, I squeezed my eyes shut. The mattress moved beneath me. I felt Edward come closer, felt the warmth of his body as he said in a low voice, "What is it?"

"This is wrong," I whispered. "You are my patient."

"It's wrong," he agreed.

My eyes flew open.

He was looking down at me with a glint in his eye. "You're sacked, Miss Maywood. Effective immediately."

I gave an indignant squeak. "You're *firing* me?"

"You said it yourself." He quirked a dark eyebrow. "I don't need a physio anymore. What I need..." Reaching out, he slowly stroked down the valley of my breasts, "is a lover."

Lover. I shivered at the word. So erotic. So suggestive. Not just of sensual delights, but emotional ones.

"You want me to be your girlfriend?" I breathed.

"No." He gave a low laugh. "Not a *girlfriend.* Just my friend. And my lover. For as long as we enjoy it." Lowering his head, he kissed my naked belly, making me shiver at the sensation of his lips and rough chin and tiny flick of his tongue against my belly button. He looked up. "This isn't a *commitment.* I won't be asking you to the movies with a box of chocolates, asking to meet your family." His eyes narrowed. "I am not *nice,* Diana. I look out for myself. I expect you to do the same." His lips lifted at the edges. "For all I know, you'll soon go back to Jason Black."

"I—"

"It doesn't matter," he cut me off. "I don't expect you to stay with me forever. It's fine," he said lightly, searching my face. "I wouldn't want to get too accustomed to you."

I am not nice, *Diana. I look out for myself. I expect you to do the same.* When a man tells you something bad about himself, that is the time to listen. I stared up at him in the shadows of the bed, hearing only my own ragged breath, my own heartbeat, as I tried to focus on his words. But I was distracted, burning hot with his naked body over mine.

Don't lie to yourself about what the end will be, Mrs. Warreldy-Gribbley had warned. *If you forget yourself and let him lure you into his sensual designs—*

But I didn't want to think about her anymore. The woman had written the book in 1910, I thought irritably. What did she know? I shut the book in my mind, locking it away forever.

And I smiled up at Edward. "Good to know," I said, matching his light tone. "I wouldn't want to get too accustomed to you either. I have things to do in life."

"Do you?" he said, sounding amused. Then, moving closer, he looked at me. My heart pounded as his breathtakingly beautiful face, just inches from mine, was illuminated in moonlight, making him look like a dark angel. "Yes," he murmured. "I think you do. You're meant for great things in life, Diana."

My lips parted, and I felt suddenly tearful for no good reason, other than that no one had ever said such a thing to me. No one, not since my mother had died—

"Great things," Edward whispered again, lowering his head to mine. His lips curved wickedly. "Starting with tonight…"

He kissed me, his hands stroking down the length of my body, slowly removing the last of my clothes, my skirt, my cotton stockings. He ran his hand appreciatively along my hips, my thighs. My breasts. He unclasped my bra so easily, he practically just looked at it to make it spring open. Dropping the flimsy blue silk off my body, he cupped one of my breasts with both hands. I sucked in my breath, my whole body taut.

He pulled away with a low curse.

"I forgot you're a virgin." He shook his head with an irritated growl. "So let me make this really clear for you. One more time. For the sake of my own conscience."

"I thought you didn't have one," I said weakly.

"This is all I can give you." His eyes met mine. "No marriage. No children. All I can offer is—this." He kissed me, feather-light, running down my bare, trembling throat, to my clavicle. I felt his hands cup my naked breasts, felt his fingers lightly squeeze the full, heavy flesh. He lowered his mouth with agonizing slowness to an aching nipple, then stopped at the last moment. He looked up at me. "Do you agree?"

As he spoke, his lips and breath brushed my taut nipple, and I shook beneath him, lost in desire, lost in pleasure, *lost*.

He was offering cheap, no-strings sex. No marriage. No children. Not even love.

So? I thought suddenly. What had love ever done for me? Only broken my heart.

This was better than love.

"Yes." I whispered, reaching for him. "Yes..."

Then his lips came down on my skin, his tongue swirling my nipple as he suckled me, and I gasped, gripping the sheets.

CHAPTER FOUR

HIS TONGUE SWIRLED hot and tight against my nipple, and I shivered beneath him. He nibbled with his teeth, drawing me more deeply into his mouth. My breast felt full and heavy and taut beneath his hands. I felt his hips grind against me.

Moving to my other breast, he squeezed the aching nipple, tasting the exquisitely sensitive nub with a flick of his tongue. He took it fully into his mouth, suckling me. And all the while, I felt the hard ridge of him between my legs.

Drawing back, he ran his hands down the sides of my body. I felt his heat and weight pressing me into the comforter and soft white pillows of the king-size bed. Unlike the soft stroke of his hands, his lips were hard, searing mine as he gave me a kiss that had no tenderness, only fierce demand.

His fingers tangled and twisted in my hair, tilting my head so he could plunder my mouth more deeply. All my memories, all my regrets, faded into the past as I dissolved into lust—so purely alive, so purely desired. I kissed him back with all the trembling pent-up desire of my whole life.

The bristles of dark hair that covered his chest and forearms and his legs—and everywhere between—brushed roughly against my naked skin. He held me with ruthless, raw masculine power.

I felt his enormous hardness between my legs, brushing against my lower belly as he moved against me. His tongue twirled around mine as he kissed me, flicking the edges of my bruised mouth before he moved lower, kissing along my throat, working his way downward. Pressing my breasts together with his hands, he thrust his tongue into the crevasse between them, and I gasped. His breath was hot against my skin as he continued to kiss downward…down my belly and then…

Abruptly, he moved up to suckle an earlobe. My nipples felt taut almost to the point of pain as I felt the brush of his muscled chest. He moved to the other earlobe, still moving his hips sensuously against mine.

"You're—teasing me," I panted accusingly. I felt his smile against my neck.

"Yes," he murmured against my skin. "I intend to make you weep."

Slowly, delicately, he lifted my palm. He kissed the hollow, then moved his head to suck each fingertip, one by one.

I'd never thought of fingers as erogenous zones but feeling the warmth of his mouth on each fingertip, the hot wet swirl of his tongue, the hard pull of his teeth, I shook beneath him. He repeated it on my other hand, delicately sucking on each finger until I was dizzy and gasping for breath.

Slowly, he moved down my body. I felt his hot lips and wet tongue against each taut, aching nipple. His tongue swirled, his hands cupping each full, heavy breast. With a gasp, I closed my eyes, gripping the comforter.

With deliberate, agonizing slowness, he again began to move down my naked body in a trail of hot kisses. My eyes flew open in the semidarkness of the bedroom when I felt his hands move low, over my hips, running lightly over my thighs. When he brushed feather-light over the hair between my legs, I audibly choked out a gasp.

He lifted his head up lazily. "Just wait."

Lowering his head to my belly button, he flicked it with his tongue, inside it, inside me.

But even as I shivered, his mouth moved down farther.

And farther.

Running his hands over the swell of my hips, he lowered his head between my legs. I felt the warmth of his breath *right there* and gave a sharp gasp, gripping his shoulders as my head tossed back.

But he made me wait. Made me *want*. He just kept moving down my legs, all the way, down to my feet. Parting my knees, he stroked the hollow of each foot, gently massaging it, causing a different kind of pleasure to spiral up my body. He pushed my legs farther apart. Stroking up my calves, he kissed the hollow beneath my knee. I gripped his shoulders, my eyes squeezed shut.

Using his shoulders, he roughly spread my thighs all the way apart.

My breathing was ragged as I gripped the comforter, trembling beneath him. I felt the heat of his breath on the tender skin of my inner thighs. Shivering, I tried to scoot away, though I wanted it so badly. He held me down firmly. His hands pressed my legs wide. He lowered his head with agonizing slowness, making me hold my breath until I thought I might faint—

I felt the hot, wet stroke of his tongue against my slick core, and gave a muffled cry. He paused, then licked me again, this time lapping me with the full width of his tongue. As my hips twisted helplessly beneath him, he held me down, forcing me to accept the pleasure as I nearly writhed with agonized need.

"Please," I whimpered, hardly knowing what I was saying. Barely realizing that I was speaking at all. *"Please."*

He gave a low laugh.

Pushing me wider, he worked me with his tongue, lapping me with the full width one moment, then using the tip to swirl tighter, ever tighter, against the hard aching center.

He slowly pushed a fingertip inside me. Then two. As I held my breath with pleasure, he stretched me wide with his thick fingers, while licking and suckling me with his tongue.

My body was on fire, my back arching from the bed. I'd lost the ability to take a full breath. I twisted beneath him, no longer trying to get away, merely to end the sweet torment. I'd never imagined it could be like this—pleasure to the point of pain— Higher—tighter—

I heard a building scream from a voice I'd never

heard before, a voice I would only later realize was mine. My eyelids half closed as I left the earth and exploded past the sun.

As I gasped for breath, Edward moved quickly, bracing himself with his hands on either side of my hips. Positioning himself between my legs, he thrust himself inside me. His full length. All at once, thick and hard, ripping through me with jarring pain.

With a choked gasp, I pushed on his hips, wanting the pain to stop. He held still inside me. Then, as my grip on his hips loosened, he slowly began to move again. He pulled back, then slowly filled me again, giving me time to grow accustomed to the size of him. He filled me, stretching me inch by inch, slowly, sensuously; and the red haze of pain turned orange, then pink, then began to bubble and fizz like champagne. My body, which had been briefly limp on the bed, began to quicken again, to grow taut and tense with new desire.

Gripping my hips with his large hands tight enough to bruise, he thrust harder, until he was riding me rough and fast. My back again began to arch off the bed as he filled me deep and hard, stretching me to my limit, and beyond....

With a curse, he abruptly pulled out. I opened my eyes, nearly hyperventilating with need.

Looking at him in the slanted moonlight on his enormous bed, I saw he'd opened a condom and was peeling it over his huge length.

"I forgot," he said grimly. "I never forget."

My mouth suddenly went dry. "Then is it possible—"

"It's fine," he growled. Leaning forward, he kissed me passionately, until I forgot to worry about anything, until I forgot my own name. "Look at me."

I did. Our eyes met as he pushed back inside me, inch by throbbing inch. I gasped. As the pleasure built, I started to close my eyes, to turn away.

"Look at me," he repeated harshly.

Against my will, I obeyed. Our eyes locked as he thrust inside me. I felt every inch of him as he filled me, then increased the rhythm, shoving harder and faster as he gripped my hips. Tension coiled low and deep inside me, building tighter and tighter.

It was shockingly intimate to watch his face. Almost more intimate, even, than having him inside me. I felt the muscles of his backside grow tense beneath my hands, tense with the strain of holding himself back so tightly. Why did he hold back? Why?

Then I knew.

For me.

He thrust roughly into me, swaying my breasts as our sweaty naked bodies slid and clung together. He thrust again, so deep he impaled me. And something inside me suddenly spiraled out of control, rising from ash like a burst of fire. I was consumed by it, then exploded like a phoenix. I screamed, and heard his answering growl, as he clutched my hips tight enough to bruise. With a hoarse cry, he filled me with one last brutal, savage thrust, then collapsed over me with a groan.

I held him in the moonlight on the bed, this powerful giant of a man who'd overwhelmed me with the sweet torment of pleasure, now weak as a kitten. Closing my eyes, I cuddled him to my body, my heart in my throat.

I'd never imagined sex was like this, never.

"See?" Still panting, Edward nuzzled my neck. His voice was filled with masculine self-satisfaction as he traced his fingertips down my cheek. "I told you."

"What?" I choked out, holding him closer, never wanting to let him go.

His dark blue eyes smiled sleepily into mine. "That I would make you weep."

Astonished, I touched my face and found he was right. He'd made me weep. It was the first time.

It wouldn't be the last.

Sunlight poured golden through the windows as Edward woke me with a kiss. "Good morning."

"Good morning," I said a little shyly, yawning. Our bodies were still naked, our limbs intertwined. I felt amazingly, blissfully sore in all the right places.

We'd made love three times last night. After the explosive first time, we'd slept in each other's arms until at midnight we'd decided we were hungry. Putting on robes, we'd gone down to the dark, empty kitchen to hunt for a snack, giggling like naughty teenagers.

Naughty indeed. One minute Edward's hand was reaching for the bread box, the next it was beneath my silk robe, and the minute after that he pushed me against the kitchen wall. The fact that we could have been discovered at any moment by Mrs. MacWhirter or the other servants just made it more dangerous. Ripping my belt loose, he'd taken me against the wall, wrapping my legs around his hips as he thrust hard and deep, until I gripped his shoulders in a silent cry. It was fast. It was rough.

It was delicious.

After a quick meal of sandwiches and cake in the dark kitchen, giggling and whispering, we'd gone back upstairs. We were both so sweaty, we decided to take a shower. I don't know how this happened, either. One minute he was shampooing my hair, and I was standing on my tiptoes, reaching up to shampoo his. He playfully flicked some lather on my nose, and in retaliation, I smacked his butt really hard. He grabbed me, and two seconds later, he was shoving me against the shower's steamy glass, murmuring words of desire against my hot, rosy skin as he made love to me beneath the scorching stream of shooting water.

I shivered, remembering. Even now, as he held me in the morning light, Edward was looking at me hungrily, and I felt my body respond.

Had he been watching me sleep, waiting for me to wake? I hoped not. I'd been dreaming about him. We'd been having a summer picnic in the garden. The sky was blue, the sun warm, and flowers were in bloom around us. He'd held me close on the blanket, and when I whispered that I loved him, his dark blue eyes had lit up. *I love you, Diana,* he'd said.

What if I'd been talking in my sleep? He would freak out if he knew. "I hope I didn't wake you up by snoring or, er…" I blushed. "…talking in my sleep."

"No," Edward growled, rolling me beneath him. It seemed he hadn't woken me to talk. "You slept like the dead. Another two seconds and you would have woken up with me inside you."

"It doesn't sound like the worst way to—" He covered my mouth with his own, thrusting smoothly inside me. He was as hard as if we hadn't made love three times already; I was as wet as if he hadn't brought me to aching, explosive climax again and again.

If the other times had been passionate or rough, now, as he took me in the golden light of morning, he was tender, even gentle. How could we still be so unsatiated, so hungry for more? I grasped his shoulders tight, digging into his skin with my fingertips, holding my breath as he pushed deeper into me, until six thrusts later we were both sweaty and crying out and clutching each other.

He pulled me close, kissing my temple.

"What you do to me..." he whispered against my sweaty skin, and my soul expanded into every inch of my body. I sighed, closing my eyes and pressing my cheek against his warm, hard-muscled chest. It felt so right to be in his arms. For the first time in my life, I wasn't thinking about the past or the future. I was exactly where I wanted to be.

It was after noon by the time we woke again. "Good afternoon," he whispered now, smiling as he kissed me.

"Good afternoon." I sighed, then stretched across the bed. "I hate to get up."

"So don't."

"I'm hungry." I smiled, then my smile faltered. "And I have a lot to pack."

"Pack?" He frowned. "For what?"

"For home."

"You're leaving?"

He sounded indignant. An unwilling laugh lifted to my lips. "You fired me."

"Ah." Relaxing, Edward looked thoughtful. "*Fired* is such a strong word. *Made redundant* is more accurate. By your own hard work, I might add." He tilted his head. "Now, you're probably asking yourself, what kind of heartless bastard would cut someone out of a job right before Christmas?"

"Um, you?"

He laughed. "You've been paid in full. While you were on your walk yesterday, I had my secretary deposit your entire promised salary—the whole year's worth."

I stared at him. "What?"

He looked amused. "You really should pay more attention to your bank account."

"You're right," I said. Tell me something I didn't know. "Well. Um. Thanks. I guess I'll go pack…"

"Don't go." He grabbed my wrist. His voice was low. "I want you to stay with me. Through the New Year, at the very least. Not as my employee, but as my—"

"Yes," I blurted out.

Snorting, he lifted a dark eyebrow. "I could have said *slave*."

I gave him a crooked grin. "Then definitely yes."

"Thank God," he said softly, smoothing tendrils of hair off my face. "One last week of holiday," his lips turned downward, "before I go back to London."

My stomach growled. Standing up, I walked

naked across the room and picked up my silk robe. I tied it around me. "What's in London?"

"My job."

"You really have to go?"

"I've been gone too long. My cousin Rupert is trying to convince the shareholders he should take my place."

"Sounds like a jerk."

"He's a St. Cyr."

"Then definitely a jerk," I said teasingly, but he didn't smile back. I hesitated. "But why does it matter?"

"What do you mean?"

I motioned around the bedroom. "You seem to have plenty of money. I figured being CEO of the family company was a sort of honorary title, you know...."

"Like a sinecure—getting paid for doing nothing?"

"I wasn't trying to insult you. But you don't seem keen to get back there. If you don't need the money, there's nothing forcing you to do it, is there?"

He scowled. "St. Cyr Global was started by my great-grandfather. I'm the largest shareholder. I have a responsibility...."

"I get it," I said, but I didn't.

Edward looked away. "Come on. Let's see about breakfast."

Mrs. MacWhirter was making bread in the kitchen, and it smelled heavenly. The housekeeper's eyebrows rose almost all the way to her white hair when she saw me still in my robe, with Edward looking tousled in a T-shirt and sweatpants that clung to his chiseled body. There could be no doubt about what we'd been up to. But she recovered quickly when Edward meekly asked if we'd missed any chance of breakfast.

"Missed? I'll say not! With everything?"

"Black tea for me, if you please, Mrs. MacWhirter. And extra tomatoes."

"Of course. And Miss Maywood?"

I found it impossible to return her gaze without blushing. "Everything, please. With extra toast and jam. Coffee with cream and sugar. Please, thank you, if you don't mind, you're so very kind…."

Edward grabbed my hand, stopping me before I could babble any further.

"We'll be in the tea room," he said firmly, and drew me away. A moment later, we were in a bright room with big windows facing the garden and beyond that, the sea. A brisk fire was going. I blinked when I saw the rose-colored carpet, the chintz pattern of the wallpaper.

"Whose room is this? You can't have designed this."

His jaw tightened. "It was my mother's."

He'd never mentioned her before. "Does she visit often?"

"She died last year," he said shortly.

"I'm so sorry—"

"Don't be. As far as I'm concerned, she died long ago. She left when I was a child. Ran off with an Argentinian polo player when I was ten."

"Oh," I breathed.

It was a good reminder of the lesson I learned as a child, he'd said. *Never depend on anyone.*

He shrugged. "Dad worked all the time, and traveled overseas. Even when he was home, he had a mean streak a mile wide." He gave me a humorless smile. "The St. Cyr trait, as you said."

My heart ached for the ten-year-old boy who'd been abandoned by his mother. Even though both my parents had died, I never had any doubt of their love for me. My heart twisted. And then I suddenly felt furious. "Your parents were selfish."

His expression froze. Turning away, he threw

himself into in an overstuffed chintz chair in front of the fire. "I was fine."

I sank into the matching chair on the other side of the tea table. "Fine? To run off and leave you? Abandon you with a mean, neglectful father?"

"Well." He gave me a wry smile. "I do wish Mum had told me the truth from the start. The day she left for Buenos Aires, she cried and said she was breaking up with Dad, not me. She promised she'd always be my mother and that the two of us would still be a family." He looked away. "But within a year, her letters and calls began to dwindle. She stopped asking me to Argentina for Christmas. Not that Dad would have let me…."

"He wanted to spend Christmas with you?"

Edward shook his head. "He went to Mustique at Christmas with his mistress du jour. He just hated Mum and didn't want to do anything nice for her. It wasn't just that. Antonio didn't want me at his house, really. He just wanted Mum."

"That must have been hard…."

He shrugged. "When I was fourteen, Mum had a new baby. She was so busy, and so far away. She quit phoning, or sending letters. It was easier just to leave me behind." He barked out a laugh. "It all happened long ago. But I wish Mum had told me from the beginning how it would be." He looked out toward the lead-paned windows, bright with afternoon sunlight. "Rather than letting me wait. Letting me hope."

"I'm so sorry," I whispered, despising all the selfish adults who'd hurt him as a child. "Who took care of you?"

"The household staff. Mrs. MacWhirter, mostly. The gardener, too. But not for long. At twelve I went to boarding school."

"Twelve?" I sputtered.

"It was good for me. Built character and all that." He sighed. "I used to get homesick for Cornwall. I'd daydream about hitchhiking back here so the old gardener could take me out fishing. He also taught me how to catch a ball, tie a reef knot. Old Gavin was great."

"You called him Old—to his face?"

"Everyone did. To distinguish him from his son. Young Gavin." He sighed. "But his children had grown and moved away to find jobs, and Old Gavin missed his grandchildren. I promised if he'd just wait, when I grew up I'd create a factory near Penryth Hall that built things for adventures, so there'd be plenty of jobs for everyone. All he had to do was stay."

"*Things for adventures?*" I queried.

"Blow darts and slingshots and canoes. Come on, I was ten."

"Did you ever do it? Create the factory?"

"No." He looked away. "Old Gavin emigrated to Canada, to be with his daughter. A few months after that, I was at boarding school. He didn't keep his promise. I don't have to keep mine."

"Oh, Edward…" I tried to reach for his hand. But he wouldn't accept either my hand or my sympathy.

"It's fine," he said roughly. "I was lucky. I've learned not to count on people. Or make promises I can't keep."

Mrs. MacWhirter came bustling noisily into the room, followed by a maid, both of them carrying trays. As they set down china cups and napkins and solid silver utensils, Edward smiled at the housekeeper. I realized that the older woman, gruff as she could be, was the closest to family he had. She poured Edward's black tea and my coffee, set down our plates and left us.

I looked down hungrily at my breakfast, with eggs, toast, beans and grilled tomato, and a type of bacon that tasted like ham. I loved it all. I slathered the buttered toast with marmalade, then took a delicious crunchy bite. We ate in silence, sitting together near the fire. Then our eyes met.

"I don't blame you for never wanting to depend on anyone," I said softly. "Why would you? People lie, or love someone else, or move to Canada. People leave you, even if they don't want to. Even if they love you." I paused. "People die."

For a moment, the only sound was the crackling of the fire. He stared at me. "You're not going to argue with me?"

I shook my head.

"I'm surprised," he said gruffly, watching me. "Most women accuse me of having no heart."

I thought of my kindhearted father, a professor, who'd died suddenly in an accident when I was in third grade, and my mother, who'd filled my life with roses and sunshine before her long, agonizing decline. They'd never have chosen to leave me, or each other. But they'd had no choice. In spite of their fervent promises. "Maybe you're right," I said in a small voice, looking down at my plate. "Maybe promises are worthless. All we have is today."

His hand took mine across the table.

"But if we live today right," he said quietly, "it's enough."

The air between us suddenly electrified, and my hand trembled beneath his. Slowly, he started to lean across the tea table....

Mrs. MacWhirter coughed from the doorway, and Edward and I pulled away, blushing like teenagers who'd just been caught kissing.

"I'm sorry to interrupt you, sir," she said, "but I wanted you to know I'm getting ready to leave. The rest of the staff has already gone."

"Fine." Edward cleared his throat. "Good. I hope you have a nice holiday."

"Yes, indeed, sir," Mrs. MacWhirter said warmly. "The staff wanted me to thank you for the extra large Christmas bonus this year. You're always so generous, but this one topped it all. I nearly fell over when I opened the card. Sophie said she's going to surprise her boyfriend and take him to the Seychelles for Christmas. I'm going to get my sister that new roof, and I'll still have some left to put by. Thank you."

"It's the least you all deserve for putting up with me," Edward said. "Especially over the last few months. I haven't always made it easy."

Her lips lifted into a smile. "You haven't been so very bad as all that. Considering all you've been through..." She hesitated. "I needn't go to

Scotland for Christmas, you know. I could stay over the holiday, if you think you might need me."

"Don't be ridiculous," he said sharply. "You've been talking about visiting your sister for months. You get the week off, as always."

"But in your current state…who will take care of you?"

"Miss Maywood."

She eyed me dubiously. "What about in the kitchen?"

"In the kitchen," he said gravely, "as in all areas."

He didn't meet my eye, and a good thing too, since I could barely keep from laughing.

"In that case…I'm off." Mrs. MacWhirter looked relieved. "Happy Christmas, Mr. St. Cyr, Miss Maywood. Take good care of him," she added with a beady glint in her eye.

"I will," I murmured, feeling new appreciation for her, now that I knew she'd been caring for Edward since he was a child.

And I kept my promise, all right. I took very good care of Edward over Christmas week. Just as he took very good care of me. We huddled in the warmest rooms of Penryth Hall, lighting a fire with a Yule log, and watched the snow rise in the chilly wind outside.

We had sex for Christmas. Sex for Boxing Day. Sex for New Year's Eve. In between, we had champagne, opened Christmas crackers, wore paper crowns and gobbled up a Christmas goose we'd prepared ourselves—Edward actually knew how to cook, somewhat to my surprise—and a great deal of trifle.

I'm not going to lie. It was a very naked week. Alone just the two of us, we barely bothered with clothes. Edward said it was more efficient that way, plus he just liked the look of me. We lit fires in every room, in every possible way.

Christmas morning, we made love beneath the tree and it was so explosive that at the critical moment, ornaments and tinsel fell on Edward's head. Edward looked up with a mix of amusement and annoyance.

"I've heard about choirs of angels singing," he grumbled, looking at the angelic item that just had landed on his back from the very top of the tree, "but this is ridiculous."

With a laugh, I pulled him back over me, and we wrapped ourselves in tinsel.

But on New Year's Eve, as all the world looked with anticipation toward the bright, shiny new year, I felt building sadness, the sense that our time was running out. I tried to ignore the feeling, telling myself I should be grateful for the magical weeks we'd spent together. But all I could feel was misery, that soon Edward would return to London, to work long hours at a job he didn't particularly like, and I would go back to California, to face the scandal I'd left behind, and see if I had the courage to try acting again. Just thinking of it made me want to cover my head with a pillow. And as for the thought of never seeing Edward again, never ever....

"Stop sighing," Edward said across the table. "I don't believe it for a second. I'm not going to fall for it again."

We were sitting in the study, at a folding table we'd moved directly in front of the fire, where for the past hour we'd been playing strip poker. Caesar the sheepdog was stretched out on a rug beside us, ignoring us, clearly disgusted by the whole thing. I sat half-naked in my chair, wearing only panties, a bra, knee socks and Edward's tie. Which probably sounds grim, where strip poker is concerned. But Edward had only his silk boxers left. He was sweating.

"Where did you learn to play like this?" he demanded, staring down fiercely at his own cards.

"Madison taught me," I said sweetly. "We used to play all the time."

His scowl deepened. "I might have known Madison was at the bottom of this."

"Yeah." I looked down at my own cards. I didn't even have a particularly good hand, but due to my confidence—and the straight flush I'd had in the last round—he believed I might. Nothing except a miracle could save him now. Madison had taught me this much about acting—how to bluff.

Madison. I missed her, in spite of everything. I'd called my stepfather on Christmas, on set in New Mexico, where he was filming the latest season of his highly regarded cable TV zombie series. I would have tried to call Madison too, except Howard let me know she'd just left for some ashram in India, to cope with her explosively public breakup with Jason.

"She could use a friend, kiddo," Howard had told me quietly.

"She doesn't want to talk to me," I'd mumbled. "She hates me."

"No, sweetie, no. Well, maybe. But I think the person she hates most right now is herself."

Edward's cell phone rang, rattling violently across the table, drawing me out of my reverie.

"Saved by the bell," I murmured. "Don't think it will save you. Those boxers will be *mine*..."

But he was no longer listening. His jaw was tight as he answered the phone. "Rupert. What the hell do you want?"

Rising to his feet, he kept the phone to his ear as he stalked back and forth across the study, barking angry words into the phone—words I didn't understand, like EBITDA, proxy fight, flip-over and poison pill. Whatever it meant, it made Edward so angry that he utterly forgot me sitting half-naked in the chair, staring up at him, wearing his tie. He just paced back and forth in front of the fire. Caesar lifted his head and watched his master walk to and fro, as bewildered and alarmed as I was.

"And I'm telling *you*," Edward bit out, "if you don't pull this together the shareholders will never forgive...no, it was *not* my fault. I set it on target. It was fine in September." He paused, then strode five steps before turning. His pace was almost a stomp as he said acidly, "Oh, I'm sorry, was it *inconvenient* to the company that I had to take a few months off when I nearly died? Even half-dead, I'm twice the man you…" He halted, grinding his teeth. "No, *you* listen to me…." A curse came from his lips that made me flinch. "If the deal is falling apart, you're the one to blame, and the board of directors will see—" He stopped. His shoulders looked so tight that I was afraid of what he might be doing to the muscles of his shoulders and spine. He ground his teeth. "I know what you're doing, you bastard, and it won't work. St. Cyr Global belongs to me…."

I couldn't listen anymore. Sliding miserably off the chair, I grabbed my clothes that had been flung so eagerly to the floor. Shivering, though I was near the roaring fire, I pulled his tie off my throat. Edward's eye caught me, now standing in front of the enormous fireplace that was taller than me, and his expression briefly lightened as his eyes approvingly traced the scarlet lace bra and panties that had been a Christmas gift. From me to him. His forehead furrowed into a frown as, without answering his smile, I turned away and silently pulled on my long cotton sweater and black knit leggings.

"I'll be there tomorrow," he snapped, and

clicked off the phone. Coming toward me, he said, "What are you doing?"

"That should be obvious," I said.

"Take your clothes back off," he said huskily, pulling me into his arms. "We're in the middle of a game. There's no reason for you to quit. You're winning."

Winning. The word made me shudder. Because when he was on the phone, talking to that man—his cousin?—Edward's voice had sounded different. Harsher. Like someone who cared about winning. At any cost.

I'd come to see another side of Edward over the past few months. Even Jason Black, the man I'd thought I'd loved, now seemed like a pale shadow of memory compared to the devilish, sexy, arrogant man who'd become the center of my life. Edward knew the best of me—and the worst. For weeks now, I'd tried not to think about how soon I'd be leaving this magical place and returning to California, to face the real world. But now...

I pulled away from his embrace, avoiding his gaze. "You're going back to London."

"That multibillion deal I told you about is falling apart," he said grimly. "I'm going first thing in the morning."

"On New Year's Day?"

"My *cousin,*" he spat out the word, "is trying to sabotage it. I've been gone too long. Once the deal's back on track, I'll get the stockholders together and see about eliminating him...."

"Eliminating?"

He snorted a laugh. "From the board of directors. What did you think I meant?"

I licked my lips. "Well..."

"You really do think the worst of me," he said, sounding amused rather than offended. "But Rupert has a wife and young children he barely sees. I'd like to free him from all the pesky duties of COO, so he could devote more time to his family."

"You could do that yourself," I pointed out.

"Ah, but I don't have a family," he said lightly. Leaning forward, he kissed my nose. "I couldn't be responsible for a houseplant."

"That's not true."

"Sadly, it is."

"What about Caesar?"

The dog lifted his head at hearing his name. Edward looked down at him affectionately. "This lazybones? You know he's technically Mrs. Mac-Whirter's dog, not mine. And she'll be back from

Scotland tomorrow. There's no help for it." Edward stared down at me grimly. "I need to go back."

In spite of his words, as I looked at his body posture, I'd never seen any man less keen to do anything.

"I understand." I kept my voice even, squaring my shoulders and trying to look calm, though I wanted to cling to him and whimper. "I'll go pack my things."

"Good." He looked distracted. Geez. It's not like I expected Edward to say he was wretchedly heartbroken, and that he'd miss me desperately, but...

I suddenly realized that was exactly what I'd expected. We'd had a torrid ten day affair, months of friendship before that, and I'd actually thought I meant something to him. In spite of the fact that he'd warned me that I wouldn't. In spite of his warnings, in spite of my promise, I'd come to care for him. Really care.

I was so stupid!

Trembling, I tried to smile. "I'll go see about the next flight to L.A." I bit my lip. "It's good timing, really. I should be thanking that cousin of yours. My stepfather invited me to spend a week on his set as an extra. It'll be fun to be a zombie. And I've heard New Mexico is beautiful...."

Edward focused on me. "What are you talking about?"

"You're going to London tomorrow."

"Yes."

I licked my lips. "So there's no point in me staying here."

"None."

"Right." I set my shoulders and tried to arrange my face into a calm, pleasant, totally unfazed expression. "That means this is goodbye."

His dark eyebrows raised. "You're abandoning me?"

"You just said there's no reason for me to stay!"

"There's no reason for you to stay at Penryth Hall," he said with almost insulting patience, "because you're *coming with me to London*."

I stared at him. In spite of his almost rude care in speaking the words, it seemed he hadn't said them carefully enough, because I still couldn't understand them.

"You want me to come with you?" I said dumbly. "To London?"

"Yes-s-s," he said, enunciating even more slowly. "To *London*."

I tried to ignore the rush of relief that went through me, the pathetic joy in my heart that he wanted me, that the moment of separation could be avoided for a bit longer. "But what on earth would I do there?"

He lifted an eyebrow. "I could hire you back as my physio."

"Come on. You can *jog* now. You don't need a physical therapist anymore."

"Then," he said huskily, "come as my full-time lover."

"I'd live in London and just—spend time with you in bed?"

"Think of it as a vacation."

"*You* won't be on vacation. You'll be working all the time."

"Not at night." He gave me a wicked grin. "I'll be your toy boy then, what do you say?" He came closer. "You'll have me all night. Isn't that what you love about me?"

I love everything about you, I wanted to say. *The way you touch me. The sound of your voice. The way you make me laugh. Everything.*

But I knew it was the last thing that he wanted to hear. It was supposed to be a physical affair, nothing more. I looked at him in the flickering firelight of his study. He was still dressed only in silk boxers from our strip poker match, and my gaze lingered at his powerful torso, hard-muscled biceps and thickly hewn thighs. Sex was enough, I told myself. It had to be enough.

"Diana?" He was staring at me. I realized I'd taken too long to respond.

"Of course that's what I love best," I said, tossing my head. "What else is there about you to love?"

"Such a heartless woman," he sighed, then drew closer. Nuzzling me, he cupped my breast through my thin cotton sweater. My nipples turned instantly hard, pressing up through the red lace of my bra, thrusting visibly against the sweater. He whispered, "Allow me to serve you, then, milady…."

Falling to his knees in front of me, Edward suckled me, pressing his mouth over my nipple. I gasped as I felt his hot mouth through the thin cotton and fillip of red lace beneath. His free hand wrapped around my other breast, then a moment later, he moved to that side.

My sweater disappeared, then the red lace

bra. With a growl of satisfaction, he lowered his mouth to my bare skin. My head fell back, my eyes closed. His lips were hot and soft, satin and steel. When he drew back, I was shivering with need, just like the first time he'd touched me. As though we hadn't been making love four times a day, every day, for the past ten days.

"So we're agreed," he murmured. Rising to his feet, he pulled me into his arms. "You'll come with me to London."

"I can't just go there as…as your sex toy," I said in a small voice, my stupid, traitorous heart yearning for him to argue with me, to tell me I meant more to him than that.

"I know." He suddenly smiled. "London has a thriving theater scene. You can live at my house as you audition for acting roles."

"Audition?" I said, trying to keep the fear from my voice.

"It's perfect." Running his hands down my back, he kissed my cheek, my neck. "By day, you pursue your dreams. At night…you'll belong to me."

Cupping my face, he kissed me, hot and demanding. I wrapped my arms around him, kissing him back recklessly, ignoring my troubled heart.

I couldn't give him up. Not yet. Not when I could still live in his world of passion and color and desire for a little while longer. I wanted to be the bold woman who wore red lace panties for her lover, and paraded around nearly naked. I wasn't ready to go back and be that invisible girl again. Not yet. I needed to be in his arms. I needed to be with him, one moment teasing each other, playing like children, and the next bursting into flame in the most adult way possible. It reminded me of the old definition of love—*friendship on fire...*

No. My eyes flew open. I cared about Edward, sure. I liked him a lot. But that wasn't the same as being in love.

I couldn't let it be.

I like him, that's all, I told myself firmly. *We have fun together. It's not a crime.*

I pulled away. "All right," I said, keeping my voice casual. "I'll come to London."

"Good," he said, with a low, sensual smile that said he'd never doubted he could convince me. Leaning me back against the poker table, he got me swiftly naked beneath the bright heat of the fire and made love to me.

And so the next morning, under the weak pink light of the dawn, I was packed up in his expensive car, along with the rest of his possessions, and driven east across the moor. Toward civilization.

CHAPTER FIVE

"WOW. YOU'RE NOT LOOKING so great."

The girl sitting beside me on one of the plastic chairs lining the hallway had a concerned look on her beautifully made-up face.

"I'm fine," I replied, trying to breathe slowly, fervently trying to believe it. It had been two months since we'd arrived in London, and I'd felt strangely queasy, almost from the day we'd arrived here. I'd thought it was from fear, and also the guilt of lying to Edward about how I actually spent my days. But today, I'd finally faced my fear. For the first time, I was actually forcing myself to stay through an audition, rather than chickening out and fleeing for Trafalgar Square like a safely anonymous tourist.

For an hour, I'd sat here in the hallway, practicing my lines in my head and waiting for them to call my name. Shouldn't the queasy feeling have gone away?

Instead, it had only increased as I waited backstage at a small, prestigious West End theater, surrounded by beautiful, professional-looking actors, who were loudly practicing their lines and doing elocution exercises, and taking no notice of me whatsoever. Except for the American girl sitting next to me.

"Are you feeling sick?" she asked now.

"Just nerves," I said weakly.

"You look like you ate a bad curry. Or else it's the flu." Wrinkling her nose, she leaned away from me ever so slightly. "My sister looked like that the first three months she was pregnant...."

"I'm fine," I repeated sharply, then swallowed, my head falling back as another wave of nausea went through me.

So much for my acting skills. Clearly not fooled, the girl looked nervously from side to side. "Oh. Good. Well. Um... Please excuse me. I have to practice my lines...over there."

Getting up, she left in a hurry, as if she'd found herself sitting next to Typhoid Mary. I couldn't blame her, because I felt perilously close to throwing up. Leaning my head against the wall, I closed my eyes and tried to breathe. I was so close to auditioning now. In a moment, they would call my name. I would speak my lines on the stage.

Then the casting agents would tell me that I sucked. It would be hideous and soul-crushing but at least I could slink home afterward and no longer be lying when I told Edward that while he was working eighteen-hour days at his office in Canary Wharf, I'd spent the day pursuing my dreams.

Just a few minutes more, and it would be over. I tried to breathe. They would probably cut me off halfway through my lines, in fact, and tell me I was too fat/thin/old/young/wrong, or just dismiss me with a curt *Thank you.* All I needed to do was speak a few lines and...

My lines. My eyes flew open as I slapped my hand on my forehead. What were my lines? I'd practiced them for two days, practiced them in the shower and as I walked through the barren garden behind Edward's lavish Kensington townhouse. I knew those lines by heart. But they'd fled completely out of my brain and...

Then I really did feel sick and I raced for the adjacent bathroom, reaching it just in time. Afterward, I splashed cold water on my face and looked at myself in the mirror. I looked pale and sweaty. My eyes looked big and afraid.

My sister looked like that the first three months she was pregnant.

Leaving the bathroom, I walked out to the hallway. Then I kept walking, straight out of the theater, until I was outside breathing fresh, cold air.

My nausea subsided a bit. The sky was dark and overcast, not cold enough to snow but threatening chilling rain.

It was the first of March, but spring still felt far away. I walked slowly for the underground station, my legs trembling.

My sister looked like that the first three months she was pregnant.

The possibility of pregnancy hadn't even occurred to me. I carefully hadn't let it occur to me. I couldn't be pregnant. It was impossible.

I stopped abruptly on the sidewalk, causing the tourists behind me to exclaim as they nearly walked into me.

Edward had gone out of his way to take precautions. But I hadn't even worried about it, because I assumed Edward knew what he was doing. He was the one who never wanted to commit to anyone, and what could be a greater commitment than a child?

But there had been a few near misses. A few

times he didn't put on the condom until almost too late. And that one time in the shower...

Feeling dazed, I walked heavily to Charing Cross station nearby and barely managed to get on the right train. I stared at the map above the seats as the subway car swayed. My cycle was late. In fact, I realized with a sense of chill, I hadn't had a period since we'd arrived in London two months ago. There could be all kinds of reasons for that. I was stressed by my half-hearted attempts at breaking into the London theater scene. I was stressed by the fact that I was lying to Edward about it. And then there was the nausea. I'd told myself my body was still growing accustomed to Greenwich Mean Time, or as the girl had suggested, I'd eaten a bad fish vindaloo.

All right, so my breasts felt fuller, and they'd been heavy and a little sore. But—I blushed—I'd assumed that was just from all the sex. The rough play at night was almost the only time I ever saw Edward anymore.

Every morning, his driver collected him before dawn to take him to his building in Canary Wharf, gleaming and modern, with a private shower and futon in his private office suite, and four PAs to service his every whim. Battling to save the deal that his cousin was trying to sabotage, he'd worked eighteen hours a day, Sundays included, and usually didn't return until long after I was in bed. Some nights he never bothered to come home at all.

But on the rest, Edward woke me up in the dark to make love to me. A bright, hot fire in the night, when his powerful body took mine with hungry, insatiable demand. Sometime before dawn, I'd feel him kiss my temple, hear him whisper, *Good luck today. I'm proud of you.* Half-asleep, I'd sigh back, *Good luck,* and then he was gone. I'd awake in the morning with sunlight slanting through the windows, and his side of the bed empty. And I would be alone.

My days in London were lonely. I missed the life we'd had in Cornwall. I missed Penryth Hall.

Everything had changed.

Was it about to change more?

Distracted by my thoughts, I almost missed my stop at High Street Kensington. I exited the underground station and then, not daring to meet the pimply sales clerk's eyes, I bought a pregnancy test from the pharmacy on the corner.

Edward had offered his driver's services to take me to auditions, but I didn't think it would do me any favors to arrive via chauffeured car, like the kept woman I'd somehow become. Plus, then I would have had to actually go to the auditions. Easier to take the underground and keep my independence—and my secrets. I didn't want Edward to feel disappointed in me, as he would if he knew I hadn't made it to a single audition in two months, in spite of all my bravado.

I hadn't wanted a driver then, but now, as I trudged up the street with my pharmacy bag tucked into my purse, the cold gray drizzle turned to half-frozen rain, soaking through my light cotton jacket, and I suddenly wished I had *someone* to look after me. Someone who would take me in his arms and tell me everything was going to be all right. Because I was scared.

I reached Edward's beautiful Georgian townhouse, with its five bedrooms and private garden, in an elegant neighborhood a few blocks from Kensington Palace. Heavily, I walked up the steps and punched the security code, then opened the front door.

"Diana?" Mrs. Corrigan's voice called from the kitchen. "Is that you, dear?"

"Yes," I said dully. No need to panic, I told myself. I'd take the pregnancy test. Once it said negative, I'd relax, and have a good laugh at my fears, along with a calming glass of wine.

"Come back," she called. "I'm in the kitchen."

"Just a minute." I went to the front bathroom. Trembling, I took the test. I waited. And waited. *Be negative,* I willed, staring down at it. *Be negative.*

The test looked back at me.

Positive.

The test fell from my numb hand. Then I grabbed it and looked at it again. Still positive. I stuffed it at the bottom of the trash, hiding it beneath the empty bag. Which was ridiculous.

Soon there would be no hiding it.

Pregnant. My teeth chattered as I stumbled slowly down the hall to the large modern kitchen at the back. Pregnant.

I looked out the big windows by the kitchen, overlooking the private garden that would be beautiful in spring, but at the moment was bleak and bare and covered with shards of melting snow.

"There you are, dear." Mrs. Corrigan, his full-time London housekeeper, was making a lemon cake. "Mr. St. Cyr just phoned for you."

"He called here?" My heart unfolded like a flower. Edward had never called me from work before. Had he somehow known I needed him, felt it in his heart?

She looked up a little reproachfully from the bowl. "He was dismayed that he couldn't reach you on your mobile."

"Um…" The sleek new cell phone he'd bought for me last month was still sitting on the granite kitchen countertop, plugged in, exactly where I'd left it two days ago. "I'll phone him back now."

My hands shook as I walked down the hall to his study, closing the door behind me. Dialing his number, I listened to the phone ring, in that distinctly British sound, reminding me I was a long way from home. And so did the fact that I needed to navigate through two different secretaries before I finally heard Edward's voice.

"Why didn't you answer your mobile?" he demanded by way of greeting.

"I'm sorry, I forgot it. I was at an audition and…" My voice trembled.

"The deal just went through."

His voice sounded so flat, it took me a moment to realize that he was calling to share good news. "That's wonderful! Congratulations!" I said brightly. My heart was pounding in my throat. "But, um, we need to talk—"

"Yes, we do," he said shortly. "There's going to be a party tonight hosted by Rupert's wife, at their house in Mayfair. Wear a cocktail dress. Be ready at eight."

Rupert's wife. Victoria. I'd met her a few times. She was mean. I took a deep breath. "I'll be ready. But something has happened today, Edward. Something really important you should know about." I paused, but he didn't say anything. "Edward?"

It took me several seconds to realize he'd already hung up. Incredulously, I stared down at my cell phone.

"Everything all right, dear?" Mrs. Corrigan said cheerily as I came out of the study.

This is all I can give you, Edward had said, the night he took my virginity. *No marriage. No children. All I can offer is—this.*

It was more true than I'd realized. Because sex was truly all he gave me now. Sex that felt almost anonymous in the dark shadows of our bed. Sex, and a beautiful house to live in while I attempted to create the acting career that was supposedly my Big Dream. Except it made me sick.

Or maybe it was the pregnancy doing that.

What would he say when he found out? Would he be furious? Indifferent? Would he think I'd somehow done it on purpose? Would he ask me to end the pregnancy?

No way. My hands unwillingly went to my slightly curved belly. Even in my shock, I already knew that I was keeping this baby. There was no other option for me.

But I was scared of his reaction.

I feared I already knew what it would be.

Mrs. Corrigan was whipping the frosting, humming merrily as I walked into the kitchen. Her plump cheeks were rosy. "Such an afternoon it is!" she sighed, looking out the windows. "Rain and more rain." She looked at me. "Would you care for some tea? Or maybe some food, you're looking skin and bone," she chided affectionately.

Skin and bone? I looked down at my full breasts, my plump hips. At my belly, which would soon be enormous. I felt another strange twinge of queasiness that I now knew was morning sickness. "Um, thanks, but I'm not hungry. Edward's taking me to a party tonight, to celebrate that his deal just went through—"

"Wonderful!"

"Yes. It is." Not so wonderful that I'd be spending time with his friends. All those bankers and their wives, and the worst of them all, Rupert and his wife, Snooty McSnotty. A low buzz of anxiety rolled through me, heavy gray clouds through my soul with lightning and rain.

And at that thought, thunder really did boom outside, so loud it shook the china cup in its saucer as the housekeeper poured me tea.

"Ooh," said Mrs. Corrigan with a shiver, "that was a good one, wasn't it?"

The rain continued all afternoon and into the evening. I paced the floor, tried to read, had to reread every page six times as my mind wandered. I managed some bread and cheese for dinner, and a little bit of lemon cake. I went upstairs and showered and dressed. I blow-dried my hair, making it lustrous and straight. I put on makeup. I put on the designer cocktail dress he'd bought me. It was tighter and skimpier than anything I'd ever worn before. Especially now. For heaven's sake, how could I not have noticed my breasts were this big?

I was ready early, at seven forty-five. Going into the front room, I sat shivering on the sofa as I waited. Outside, the traffic had dissipated, and the street was dark. Beneath the rain, puddles shone dull silver against the street lights. I waited.

It wasn't until an hour later, almost nine, that I heard the front door slam. He ran upstairs, calling my name.

"I'm in here."

"Sitting in the dark?" he growled. Coming into the front room, he clicked on a light, glowering at me. "What are you doing, Diana?"

I blinked, squinting in the light. "I just didn't notice."

"Didn't notice?" Edward looked handsome, British and rich, a million miles out of my league in his tailored suit and tie. A warrior tycoon ready to do battle by any means—with his fists, if necessary.

But his eyes looked tired. I suddenly yearned to take him in my arms, to make him feel better. But I doubted my news would do that.

"Edward." I swallowed. "We need to talk…."

"We're late," he said shortly. "I need to change."

Turning, he raced back up the stairs, his long legs taking the steps three at a time. He seemed in foul temper for a CEO that had just made a billion-dollar deal. In record time, he returned downstairs, wearing a designer tuxedo, and looking more devilishly handsome than any man should look. I felt a sudden ache in my heart. "You look very handsome."

"Thanks." He didn't return the compliment. Instead, his lips twisted down grimly as he held out my long black coat, wrapping it around my shoulders. His voice was cold. "Ready?"

"Yes," I said, although I'd never felt less ready in my life. We left the house, getting into the backseat of the waiting car.

"How was your audition today?" he asked abruptly as his driver closed the car door.

As the driver pulled the car smoothly from the curb, I looked at Edward, suddenly uneasy. I licked my lips. "It was…surprising, actually."

"You're lying," he said flatly. "You didn't even go."

"I did go," I said indignantly. "I just didn't stay, because… Wait." I frowned. "How do you know?"

"The director is a friend of mine. He was going to give you *special consideration.*" Edward glared at me. "He called me this afternoon to say you never even bothered to show. You lied to me." He tilted his head. "And this isn't the first time, is it?"

Lifting my chin, I looked him full in the face. "I haven't done a single audition since we got here."

He looked staggered. "Why?"

I tried to shrug, to act like it didn't matter. "I didn't feel like it."

His jaw tightened. "So you've lied to me for the last two months. And every morning before I left for work, I wished you good luck… I feel like a fool. Why did you lie?"

As the car wove through the Friday evening traffic on Kensington Road, I saw the Albert Memorial in Kensington Gardens, the ornate monument to Queen Victoria's young husband whom she'd mourned for forty years after he died. I took a deep breath. "I didn't want to disappoint you."

"Well, you have." His jaw went tight as he looked out at the passing lights of the city reflected in the rain. We turned north, toward Mayfair. "I didn't take you for a liar. Or a coward."

It was like being stabbed in the heart. I took a shuddering breath.

"I'm sorry," I whispered. "Why didn't you tell me the director was your friend?"

"I wanted you to think you'd gotten the part on your own."

"Because you think I can't?"

He shook his head grimly. "You hadn't gotten a single role. I thought I could help. I didn't tell you because…" He set his jaw. "It just feels better to be self-made."

"How would you know?" I cried.

I regretted the words the instant they were out of my mouth. Hurt pride had made me cruel. But as I opened my mouth to apologize, the car stopped. Our door opened.

Edward gave me a smile that didn't meet his eyes. "Time to party."

He held out his arm stiffly on the sidewalk. I took it, feeling wretched and angry and ashamed all at once. We walked into the party, past a uniformed doorman.

Rupert St. Cyr, Edward's cousin, had a lavish mansion, complete with an indoor pool, a five-thousand-bottle wine cellar, a huge gilded ballroom with enormous crystal chandeliers hanging from a forty-foot ceiling and very glamorous, wealthy people dancing to a jazz quartet.

"Congratulations!"

"You old devil, I don't know how you did it. Well done."

Edward smiled and nodded distantly as people came up to congratulate him on the business deal. I clutched his arm as we walked toward the coat room.

"I'm sorry," I whispered.

"I'm sorry I ever tried to help you," he said under his breath.

"I shouldn't have lied to you." I bit my lip. "But something happened at the audition today, something that you should…"

"Spare me the excuses," he bit out. He narrowed his eyes. "This is exactly why I usually end love affairs after a few weeks. Before all the lies can start!"

I stopped, feeling sick and dizzy. "You're threatening to break up with me? Just because I didn't go to auditions?"

"Because you lied to my face about it," he said in a low voice, his eyes shooting sparks of blue fire. "I don't give a damn what you do. If you don't want to act, be a ditchdigger, child minder, work in a shop. Stay at home and do nothing for all I care. Just be honest about it."

"Auditioning is so hard," I choked out. I knew I wasn't doing myself any favors trying to explain but I couldn't help it. "Facing brutal rejection, day after day. I have no friends here. No connections."

His eyes narrowed as he stared at me. "You wish you were back in L.A. Is that what you're saying?"

His expression looked so strange, I hardly knew what to say. "Yes. I mean, no…."

Beneath the gilded chandeliers of the ballroom, Edward's expression hardened. So did his voice. "If you want to go, then go."

I shriveled up inside.

Turning, he left the coat room, leaving me to trail behind him.

"Edward!" I heard a throaty coo, and looking up, I saw Victoria St. Cyr coming toward us. "And Diana. What a pleasant surprise." Insultingly, she looked me up and down, and my cheeks went hot. My cocktail dress that had seemed so daring and sexy suddenly felt like layers of tacky trash bags twisted tightly around my zaftig body, especially compared to the elegantly draped gray dress over her severely thin frame. She bared her teeth into a smile. "How very…charming that you're still with us. And surprising."

Things only went downhill from there.

I did not fit into Edward's world. I felt insecure and out of place. Clutching his arm, I clung to him pathetically as he walked through the party. Even as he drank short glasses of port with the other men, and traded verbal barbs with his cousin, I tried to be part of the conversation, to act as if I belonged. To act as if my heart weren't breaking.

And Edward acted as if I weren't there, holding his arm tightly. Finally, my pride couldn't take it.

"Excuse me," I murmured, forcing my hands off his arm. "I need a drink."

"I'll get it for you," Edward said politely, as if I were a stranger, some old lady on the subway.

"No." I held up my hand. "I, um, see someone I need to talk to. Excuse me."

Was that relief I saw in his eyes as I walked away?

Awkwardly, I glanced toward Victoria St. Cyr and her friends standing by the dance floor. Turning the other way, I headed toward the buffet table. At least here I knew what to do. Grabbing a plate, I helped myself to crackers, bread, cheese—anything that promised to settle this sick feeling in my belly.

Was there any point in telling Edward I was pregnant, when it was clear he was already thinking up excuses to end our relationship?

"It won't last."

Victoria stood behind me, with two of her friends.

I stared at her. "Excuse me?"

"Don't mind her," one of the friends said. "She's not used to seeing Edward with a girlfriend."

Girlfriend made it sound like we were exclusive. Which we weren't. Well, obviously I was not dating anyone else. Was he?

My breath caught in my throat as I suddenly looked at all his late nights in a brand new light. The nights he hadn't even come home, when I'd assumed he was at work…could he have been with someone else? He'd never promised me fidelity, after all. I hadn't received a single word of commitment or love. In fact, he'd promised me the opposite.

"I wouldn't say I'm his girlfriend," I said thickly.

Victoria pounced. "What are you then?"

"His, um, physical therapist."

They all stared at me, then burst out laughing.

"Oh, is that what they're calling it now," one said knowingly.

"It's true." At least it used to be true. "Edward was in a car accident in September…"

"That's right." Victoria St. Cyr looked at me thoughtfully. Diamond bangles clacked over the music of the nearby quartet as she held up her hand. "Doesn't that all make you worry?"

"What?"

"Edward's accident." She sighed. "He was so in love with that American maid who worked at a nearby house." She looked me over insultingly. "She looked rather like you, in fact. When she fell pregnant, he helped her leave London and flew her all over the world for a year. But when she had the chance to marry the father of her baby, she dropped Edward without a thought."

"The other man was a Spanish duke," her friend added, as if that explained everything.

"Edward actually tried to blackmail her into leaving her new husband—and her baby. Fortunately, the car flipped down the hill. But if the Duke and Duchess of Alzacar had pressed charges, Edward would be in jail." Shaking her head, she said coldly, "He *should* be in jail. Rupert should be CEO."

Did she think this new knowledge would devastate me? "I know all that," I said coldly, though I was shaking. "And you're wrong. Whatever mistakes Edward made in the past, he deserves to lead St. Cyr Global. He'd never sink a billion-pound deal like his cousin tried to do." I drew myself up. "He's twice the man your husband is."

Victoria stared at me dangerously.

"Your loyalty is adorable," she said softly. "But let me offer you a little friendly advice."

Friendly? Right. I said guardedly, "Yes?"

"I understand your attraction. Truly, I do. The night I met Edward, I wanted him so badly, I would have done anything to get into his bed. *Anything.*" Her lips pursed. "Luckily I met Rupert before any damage could be done."

"Your point?"

Her thin lips curled. "Edward is poison for women. You'll see. He keeps a lover just long enough to use her body and break her heart before he tosses her in the rubbish bin. How long have you two been together now? Two months? Three?" She shook her head with a pitying sound. "You're *long* past your sell-by date. Here." She pushed a card into my hands. "Call me when you need a shoulder to cry on."

And she swept past me grandly, her entourage trailing behind her.

Numbly, I looked down at the embossed card. It was like a business card, only gilded and elegant and clearly for society. It was the craziest thing I'd ever seen.

Crumpling the card into a ball, I shoved it in my purse. Even living among the sharks of the entertainment industry hadn't prepared me for this. Edward's family was *awful*. No wonder he'd been a sitting duck for the first reasonably kind-hearted person he met—that American girl he hadn't wanted to let go. Because he loved her so much.

While he was ready to dump me for a white lie I'd told, just because I'd wanted so desperately for him to think the best of me.

Turning blindly from the buffet, I ran into a brick wall. Edward was standing behind me. I wondered how long he'd been there.

"Having a good time?" he asked, his face inscrutable.

"No," I choked out.

"It might be better with champagne."

"I don't want any." I looked up at his handsome face. Was he already trying to figure out how best to end our relationship? How to let me down easy, and without a fuss?

I wanted him to love me. I wanted him to hold me close and never let go. Everything he'd told me—from the beginning—would never happen. Stupid. So stupid!

My voice was nearly a sob. "I just want to go home."

For a long moment, Edward just looked at me. All around us in the ballroom, beautiful, glamorous people were laughing and talking, celebrating, and a few had started dancing to the music from the quartet. But as he looked into my tearful eyes, for a split second it was as if the two of us were alone again. Just like at Penryth Hall.

"All right," he said quietly. Taking my hand, he pulled me from the ballroom, stopping for my coat. His driver collected us at the curb.

The streets of London seemed darker than usual. The rain had stopped, and the clouds had lifted. The night was frosty and soundless.

We walked into his dark, silent house after he punched in the alarm code. I started to go up the stairs. He stopped me.

"I never told you," he said huskily, pulling me into his arms, "how beautiful you looked tonight."

My heart went faster. "I did?"

"The most beautiful woman there by far." Pulling me closer, he twirled a long tendril of my hair around his finger and murmured, "I was glad when you left to get a drink, because the other men were flirting with you so indecently I thought I'd have to punch them."

"They were flirting with me?" I said dumbly. I had no memory of any of this alleged flirting, or of any of the men who'd surrounded us. I just remembered clinging to Edward's arm like a silent idiot.

"Any man would want you." His hand traced up my shoulder, my neck. "You're the most desirable woman I've ever known."

"More than the woman you loved in Spain?" I heard myself blurt out.

His hand grew still. His ice-blue eyes met mine. "Why do you say that?"

I swallowed. But I couldn't back down now. "Victoria told me you took care of her for a year, helping her when she was pregnant. After she married someone else, you still loved her. You wouldn't let her go. You were willing to die for her." I stopped.

"So?" He spoke without apology, and without explanation. As if he owed me neither. It made my heart turn to glass.

I took a deep breath. "Is it true she looked like me?"

His dark eyebrows lowered. "Victoria said that?"

"Yes."

"She was guessing." His lips creased in a humorless smile. "She never met Lena. But it happens she's wrong. You look nothing alike."

I exhaled. Then I shivered. *Lena.* So that was the other woman's name. "What made you love her so much?"

His eyes narrowed. "Why do you keep pushing?"

"Because I..."

I froze.

Because I wanted to know what special quality this woman had had, that had made Edward love her so much, when he couldn't even love me a little. Had she been pretty? Had she been wise? Was it the sound of her voice or the scent of her perfume?

I wanted to know because at my deepest core, I yearned for him to love me the same way. I yearned for him to want to be with me. To stay with me. Raise a child with me.

I was in love with him, and wanted him to love me back.

My infatuation with Jason had been nothing, a schoolgirl crush, compared to what I felt for Edward, the man I'd healed, the man I'd shared a home with, the man who'd teased me and encouraged me and demanded I follow my dreams. The man who'd taken my virginity and shown me what physical love could be. The man whose child I now carried deep inside me.

I was in love with Edward.

Desperately.

Stupidly.

"Diana?"

I took a deep breath. "I was just curious, that's all." I gave him a weak smile. "After hearing Victoria talk about her. What made Lena so different?"

"Different?" Moonlight from the window caught the edge of his face, leaving his eyes in shadow. "Lena wasn't different. She was ordinary, really. But she acted helpless, as if I were the only one who could save her. She made me think…I could be her hero." His cruel, sensual lips twisted up at the edges. "Me. Isn't that hilarious? But I almost believed it. I took care of her for months, asking nothing in return. Until she suddenly left me for the Spanish bastard who'd abandoned and betrayed her."

"That's it? She acted helpless?" *I could be helpless,* I thought wildly. I felt helpless right now, looking at him, fearing there was nothing I could do to make him love me or want our baby.

He shrugged. "I thought I deserved her. That I'd earned her."

I blinked. "You can't *earn* someone's love. That's not how it works."

He gave a harsh laugh. "I've heard the words *I love you* from so many women…"

"You have?" I whispered. No one had ever spoken those words to me, except for my family.

"…but words are meaningless. Cheap. Women have said it after they've only known me a few hours—in bed. They barely knew *me* at all. They were just trying to trap me, to make me do something I didn't want to do. To *own* me."

"You mean, make you commit?"

"Exactly." He gave me a crooked grin, then looked away. "But I always imagined love to be an action, not a word. If I loved someone, I wouldn't say it, I'd show it. I'd take care of her, putting her needs ahead of my own. I'd put my whole soul into making her happy…." He cut himself off with a harsh laugh, clawing back his hair. "But what the hell do I know? I've never found love like that. So I gave up on it. And I've been happier ever since."

"I don't believe that," I said softly, looking at the stark emotion in his eyes. "I'm sorry that woman hurt you, but you can't live the rest of your life closed off from love."

"You're wrong," he said flatly.

Clutching my hands into fists at my sides, I whispered, "Do you still love her?"

He choked out a laugh. "*Love* her? No. It all seems a million years ago. I was a different person then. I'm leaving them to it. The Duke and Duchess of Alzacar are happy together, with their fat, happy baby, happily married in their big castle in happy, happy Spain. I wish them every happiness."

His voice had an edge to it. A darkness. I searched his handsome face. "You're sorry you tried to kidnap her…Aren't you?"

"I'm sorry I ever let myself care in the first place," he said coldly. "I should have known better than to think I could be any woman's hero. It's not in my nature. Now…I know who I am. Selfish to the core. And glad. My life is completely within my control."

Looking up at him, my glass heart broke into a thousand shards, each of them sharp as ice. "So you'll never have a wife—no child—no family of any kind?"

"I told you from the beginning," he said harshly. "Those are things I do not want. Not now. Not ever." With a deep breath, he took a step toward me. Gently, he cupped my cheek with his hand. "But I do want this. *You*. We can enjoy each other. For as long as the pleasure lasts."

His palm was warm and rough against my cheek, and I suddenly felt like crying. "It could be more. You have to know—"

He was already shaking his head grimly. "Don't do this to me, Diana. Let this be enough. Don't ask for more than I can give. Please. I'm not ready to let you go. Not yet—"

Pulling me tight against his hard-muscled body, he kissed me passionately in the shadowy stair-well of the Kensington townhouse.

I knew I should stop him, to force him to listen, to tell him the two things that were causing such anguish—joy, terror, desperate hope—in my heart.

I loved him.

I was pregnant with his baby.

But I was scared the moment I told him, our relationship would end. He'd see me and the child

I carried both as unwanted entanglements. Because he'd already made up his mind about what he wanted. And what he didn't want.

He wasn't going to change.

Holding him tightly, I returned his kiss. Tears streaming unchecked down my cheeks, adding salt to the taste. His lips gentled as he pressed me back against the wall of the stairwell. My head fell back as he kissed down my throat. I gasped, trembling, caught between desire and the agony of a breaking heart. How could I realize I loved him, only to lose him the same night? Blood rushed in my ears like a rhythmic buzz.

Edward pulled away with a curse, and I realized the buzz was actually his phone ringing. But who would call him so late? A business emergency? A secretary?

A mistress?

No. Surely not. But we'd never promised fidelity. He'd promised only pleasure.

"It's not me," he said shortly, looking at his phone.

Frowning, I reached down for my tiny purse that had dropped to the floor, and saw it was actually my new phone ringing. But other than Edward, the only person who knew the number was my stepfather, who'd just wrapped up production in New Mexico.

I stared down at the caller ID.

"It's Jason," I breathed.

"Black?" Edward's scowl deepened. "Why is he calling you?"

"I have no idea."

"Has he done it before?" he bit out, almost unwillingly.

I shook my head. "Something must be wrong... Oh my God." Images of Howard or Madison hurt flashed in front of my terrified eyes. Turning away, I answered anxiously, "Jason?"

"Diana?"

"Why are you calling me?"

"I'm in California... I got the number from Howard."

"What's happened? Is someone hurt?"

"Yeah. Someone's hurt."

I held my breath.

"I am," he said quietly. "I made a horrible mistake."

I frowned. "What do you mean, you made a mistake?"

Edward had been glowering beside me. But at this, he turned on his heel without a word. I watched him stalk up the staircase. Was he mad at me for answering a call in the middle of our kiss? But that wasn't fair. He was the one who'd picked up his phone first.

"I shouldn't have cheated on you," Jason said on the phone. "I should have known we'd get caught. Even at night, there's always people around the Eiffel Tower. I have so many regrets. I should have…" His voice trailed off. "You know Madison and I broke up."

"I know," I said gently.

He exhaled. "Is there any way you can ever forgive me?"

"Sure."

He paused. "Really?"

I realized somewhat to my own surprise that I'd forgiven and forgotten long ago. The way I felt for Edward now, all the angst over Jason seemed a million years ago. It didn't matter. As Edward had said—I was a different person then.

"I forgave you a long time ago…." I said quietly.

"Oh?" he said hopefully.

"Because I'm in love with Edward now."

"Oh," he sighed.

I changed the subject. "But is there any chance that you and Madison...?"

"Nah. She disappeared to India when we broke up. Now I heard she's in Mongolia doing some independent film, out on some steppe in the middle of nowhere, no makeup trailer, no catering, getting paid at scale."

"Seriously?" That didn't sound like her at all.

"Crazy, right? Must be a nervous breakdown or something. At least, that's what I suggested when I was interviewed last week for *People* magazine."

He was giving interviews about Madison, suggesting she'd had a nervous breakdown? I didn't approve of that at all. I thought of Edward, waiting for me upstairs. "If that's all you called about..."

"No. Here's why I called. I'm costarring on a web series. It's just a side project, a spin-off to promote my movie sequel coming out next summer. But the lead actress just ducked out an hour ago to go back to rehab." He paused. "I thought of you."

"You...what?" I said faintly.

"Don't get too excited. The pay is next to nothing. But the movie has a large cult following, and good visibility. So even though it's just on the web, it could help you get the attention of agents….”

As he continued to speak, I stood in the dark foyer, swaying. I felt lightheaded.

“…and you wouldn’t even have to audition. I have that much pull, at least.” He paused. “Diana? You still there?”

“I just can’t believe it,” I whispered. My hand tightened on the phone. “You’re calling out of nowhere to offer me my dream job?”

“Dream job?” He laughed “Oh man. If a shoe-string web series is your dream, you need bigger dreams.” He added apologetically, “It’s not glamorous, either. The character is pregnant. You’d need to wear padding….”

I put my hand against the wall to brace myself. “Are you kidding?” *Pregnant?* Was it fate telling me to go? I said almost tearfully, “Why are you doing this?”

“Well, I owe you, Diana,” he said quietly. “After all I put you through, it seemed the least I could do. Plus,” he added, “I’d rather work with you than some no-name nobody. Will you come?”

I thought again of Edward upstairs, waiting for me, and my heart twisted. “I’m not sure….”

“I understand,” he said dryly. “Edward doesn’t

seem like the California type." He paused. "It's up to you. But if you can get here within two days, the role is yours."

When I hung up the phone, the house was silent and dark. Mrs. Corrigan had gone to bed long ago, before we even got home from the party. It was the first time I'd been downstairs like this, with Edward up in our bedroom. Usually I was the one to sleep alone.

California. The memory of home came back to me. Sunshine. The ocean. The scent of roses in my mother's garden. I could have my dream job there, with my friends and family around me, raising my baby....

Except this wasn't just my baby. It was *our* baby. And no matter how scared I was, I had to tell Edward about it. I had to at least give him the chance to be part of our lives. And tell him I loved him. Right now.

But as I slowly went up the stairs, my heart was in my throat.

A baby. I gripped the slender oak handrail as I climbed, each shaking step echoing across the dark house. *A sweet, precious baby.* Would he be a little boy with Edward's eyes? An adorable little girl with his smile?

Then I remembered my promise.

This is all I can give you, he'd said. *No marriage. No children. All I can offer is—this. Do you agree?*

An ache lifted to my throat. I was kidding myself if I thought Edward would be happy about this. He didn't want my *love*. He didn't want my *child*. He wanted convenient sex, and to leave if it got complicated.

I covered my mouth with my hand. *Please let him be happy about my news. Give me the chance to show him how to love again....*

My legs shook as I walked down the dark hallway. I stopped at our bedroom door.

"You've kept me waiting." Edward's voice was accusing from the shadows. "Come to bed, Diana."

Come to bed. I swallowed. Clenching my trembling hands at my sides, I went forward.

As my eyes adjusted to the dim light of the bedroom, I saw the large shape of him, lying on the bed. His long legs were crossed, his arms folded beneath his head as he stared up at the ceiling. He was still fully clothed in his tuxedo, with only his tie loosened.

"How is Jason?" he said coldly, still staring up at the ceiling.

I stopped. The two men were not exactly close friends. More like rivals, really, though I had no idea what they might be rivals about. I said haltingly, "He's all right."

"I bet." With a low laugh, Edward sat up on the bed. He turned to face me. The hard lines of his body and face were in shadow, but I saw the glitter of his eyes. "So he made a big mistake, did he?"

"He felt bad about cheating on me," my voice stumbled awkwardly, "so he called me to offer me a role. It's nothing big, just a web series. But I can have the role without having to audition, as long as I'm there in two days."

"How perfect. For both of you." He rose to his feet, slowly, like a giant rising in front of me. "Do you want me to help you pack?"

My lips parted at the coldness of his tone. "I don't want to leave you—"

"It's exactly what you want," he said acidly. "Go back to California, with all your industry connections. Jason Black is dying to have you back, so much he's obligingly dug up an acting job for you. Everything you want has fallen into your lap. There's nothing left to do but give you a goodbye kiss."

Every woman Edward had trusted had abandoned him, lied to him. But I would not. "I don't want to go. Because—"

He lifted a dark eyebrow and said mockingly, "Because?"

My spine straightened, and I forced myself to say it, simply, clearly, with every syllable full of equal parts anguish and hope. "Because I'm in love with you, Edward."

The effect was immediate.

Dropping his hands, he staggered back. His eyes looked wild in the shadowy light. He took a step toward me. Then stopped.

"I want to stay," I whispered, almost begging. "Please give me a reason to stay. Tell me I have a chance with you."

I heard his intake of breath. "Diana…" He caught himself. His jaw grew tight. "No."

"You don't want me," I said miserably.

"Of course I want you," he said fiercely. Then he looked away. "I just know how this will end." With a low curse, he yanked off his loosened tuxedo tie. "I should have broken this off weeks ago. Before we left Cornwall. But I couldn't." He looked at me, and I thought I saw a sheen of bewilderment in his eyes, even grief. "And this is the result. Pain for us both."

"Don't you have any feelings for me at all?" I choked out.

He stepped back. The short distance between us suddenly became wide. "I care about you." I saw the smudges of shadows beneath his eyes. He took a breath. "In fact I'm afraid, if I let myself, I could fall in love with you, Diana."

Joy leapt in my heart. "Edward—"

"But I won't let it happen," he said flatly. "I won't let myself love you."

The cut was so sudden and savage that my breath choked off and a sound came from my lips like a whimper.

His eyes glittered. "Love is a suckers' game, Diana. I've told you that all along. The only way to win is not to play. I've learned it the hard way."

But beneath his rough voice, I thought I heard something else. Vulnerability. He was holding himself together by brute force.

"Please don't do this," I said tearfully. "Don't."

Edward looked down at me almost wistfully. "We both know you haven't been happy in London. It was just a matter of time."

I couldn't argue with that, no matter how much I wished I could. As I stood beside the enormous bed where he'd given me such pleasure in the darkness, every night for the past two months, I felt Edward's emotional and physical withdrawal, as plainly as if someone had pulled a coat off my body. I hadn't even realized it had been wrapped around my shoulders until it was suddenly gone and I felt the chill blast of winter.

Reaching into the closet, he pulled out my old suitcase. Tossing it on our bed, he calmly started dumping my clothes into it. As I watched him, aghast, he finished packing in just three minutes. "If I've missed anything, I'll have it sent to you in California."

"You're tossing me out."

His eyes held no expression. "I'm saying good-bye."

But I still hadn't told him my secret—our precious, precious secret, due in September. "Wait. We still have to talk." I took a deep breath and tried desperately, "There's something more I have to tell you—"

"We've talked," Edward said. "And now we're done." Going to the window, he opened the blinds and looked out at the elegant street, dark and quiet with all the expensive townhouses tucked in for the night, sleeping cheek by jowl in the moonlight. Pulling his phone from his pocket, Edward called his driver. Hanging up, he glanced back at me as if I were a stranger.

"Nathan will be here in five minutes to take you to the airport. My jet is at your disposal, and will take you back to where your dream career and dream man await." His lips twisted. "Thank you for your assistance with my recovery." Edward held out his hand. "I will be glad to recommend you to anyone who needs a physiotherapist in the future."

Bewildered, I took his hand. He shook it once, briskly, as if we'd only just been introduced. He started to pull away. Desperately, I tightened my hand. "Come with me to California."

His lips curved. "And what would I do there?"

"Whatever you want!"

He shook his head. "St. Cyr Global is headquartered in London. The company is my responsibility. I was born to it...."

"And you hate it," I said tearfully. "Every single minute."

He looked down at me, and an expression of

pain crossed his eyes. "It was fun while it lasted, Diana," he said quietly. "But there is no reason for us to ever see each other again."

"No reason? Are you crazy? I just told you I loved you!"

His expression hardened. "Do you expect me to change my whole life for the sake of a few cheap words?"

"Cheap?" My knees trembled from the emptiness I felt inside. It suddenly threatened to devour me, with the help of its friends, grief and despair. "I want to be with you forever. I love you, Edward," I whispered. "We could build a home together, a future." I lifted my tearful gaze to his. "We could have a child—"

My throat closed when I saw him flinch.

"Sorry. What I want," he said quietly, "is a clean break." He closed my suitcase with a snap.

"But there can't be." To my horror, my voice came out in a whimper. I wiped my eyes hard. "There will always be a connection between us now. Because you have to know that I…"

"For God's sake, stop it!"

"But I…"

"Not another word! If you won't go, I will." I had a brief view of his pale, stricken face as he rushed past me. Then he was gone, disappearing through the door in a few strides of his long legs.

I stared after him in shock. I heard the echo of the front door slamming downstairs. I looked out the window, and numbly watched Edward disappear down the street, walking out of my life forever.

A sob came from the back of my throat. I leaned against the window, my hand outstretched across the cold glass. Edward hadn't even given me the chance to tell him about the baby. Just telling him I *loved* him had made him run.

Just as I'd always known it would. Though I'd tried so hard not to know.

Through the blur of my tears, I saw a black sedan silently pull up to the curb in front of the house. Nathan, coming to take me to the airport.

I finally understood why Edward had ended our relationship. Why he'd been so determined not to love me.

It was so he'd never have to feel like this.

"Are you ready, madam?" I heard the driver's voice at the door. "Shall I bring your suitcase down?"

My hand closed to a fist against the window.

Turning slowly, I gave him a shake of my head. "I'll do it myself."

"Very good, madam."

Squaring my shoulders, I wiped my eyes. I'd thought I could teach Edward something about love. Instead, he'd taught me.

Love is a suckers' game. The only way to win is not to play.

With a deep breath, I picked up my suitcase. I'd never weep over Edward again, I vowed. All that mattered now was our baby. No.

My baby.

CHAPTER SIX

"OUT HERE AGAIN?"

Looking up, I smiled when I saw my stepfather in front of the pink bougainvillea of the garden.

"I had the morning off," I replied. "Jason's coming to pick me up in an hour."

"Always so busy." Howard gave a mock sigh. "I should have gotten you to work as a zombie when I had the chance."

"Sorry." My smile lifted to a grin. "You'll have to ask my agent now."

The web series had been as good a launch as Jason had thought it would be. In just four-and-a-half months, I'd started to have a real career. I wasn't a movie star like Madison—not even close—but it turned out I had lots of friends who were anxious to see me succeed for no other reason than that they liked me. I had already expanded into commercials, doing character roles and bit parts on television shows. It was enjoyable at times, at other times mind-numbingly boring.

If it wasn't quite the ecstatic dream I'd thought it would be, it at least had given me something to do after I left my real dream behind in London.

Or to be more accurate, he'd left me.

"Must be hard to be so popular," Howard grumbled. Then, as he looked around, a smile spread across his tanned, wrinkled face. "You've made the garden come to life again. It's exactly how Hannah had it."

"Thanks." I leaned back on my haunches, brushing dirt off my gardening gloves as I surveyed the red and yellow roses. At nearly seven months' pregnant, my belly was so large now that I had to brace myself so I didn't lose balance and topple over.

For the past four-and-a-half months, since I returned to California, I'd lived in my childhood bedroom at Howard's house, a white colonial in Beverly Hills. Whenever I wasn't working, I spent time in my mother's old garden behind the house. In April, I'd enjoyed feeling the sunlight on my face, and now it was late July, I relished the cool shade.

I was home, I told myself. I didn't let myself think about Cornwall anymore, or how happy I'd been at Penryth Hall.

I looked up gratefully at my stepfather. "Thanks for letting me stay here so long. When I asked to visit, you had no idea I'd be moving in permanently," I added, only half joking.

"Listen." He reached out to pat my shoulder. "Every single day I have you here, with a grandbaby on the way, is a blessing." Howard looked wistfully at the roses. "You've started a new career, a new life," he said gruffly. "Your mother would have been so happy about the baby. And so proud of you, Diana."

I felt a lump rise to my throat. "Thanks, Howard."

Funny to think now that I hadn't always liked him. I hadn't wanted anyone to replace my dad, and the two men were so different. My dad had been quiet and studious, caring and careful. Howard Lowe was brash and loud, and never afraid to yell—especially at actors—or start a fight.

But beneath his bluster, Howard had loved my mother more than life, and he'd taken me under his wing from the beginning, when I was a sad eleven-year-old, bookish and quiet compared to his own daughter Madison, the result of his earlier short marriage to an actress.

Swallowing, I looked from the pinks and reds

and yellows of the roses, to the more exotic flowers beneath wide cypress, pine and palm trees. "You've been so kind to me. I feel bad, with Madison giving you the silent treatment for it...."

He made a dismissive gesture. "Who's to say she is? She's busy in Mongolia. And if she's mad that I'm letting you stay here, she'll have to get over it. We're family."

I shook my head. "She'll never forgive me for ruining her relationship with Jason."

"Hush. If it was so easy to ruin, it wasn't much of a relationship." He patted my arm. "I'm glad you're here, Diana. Don't rush into leaving. Especially with Jason Black. I don't think much about a man who keeps changing his mind which sister he wants to marry."

"Howard, you know Jason and I are just friends!"

"Sure, I know that. I'm just not sure he does."

I sighed. After we'd wrapped the web series, Jason had taken me out often, whenever he had time off from the superhero movie he was filming in Century City. After the scandal of last year, the paparazzi had a field day with this latest development, and they'd followed us constantly, photographing us doing boring things like drinking lattes at a café. Last week we'd been on the cover of multiple celebrity gossip magazines. *Madison Lowe Love Triangle*, one headline screamed. *Madison's Pregnant Stepsister Strikes Back with Baby Daddy Jason Black!*

I'd writhed when I read it. So much for trying to avoid the paparazzi, and maintain a dignified silence.

"Just tell everyone it's mine," Jason had urged. "It will be, after we're married."

"We're not getting married, Jason," I'd said, rolling my eyes. "We're friends. Just friends."

But did he really accept that?

I sighed in irritation, remembering. "Love is a suckers' game," I grumbled to Howard.

I suddenly realized who I was quoting. I didn't love Edward anymore. Instead, I'd become him.

"Okay, okay." Howard held up his hands. "Whatever. I'm staying out of it. But look." His expression turned ferocious, his gray eyebrows bushy and fierce. "I don't know what the deal was with your baby's father, or why you decided it would be a mistake to tell him about the pregnancy…."

"I don't want to—"

"Yeah, I know you don't like to talk about it. But take it from an old man. Life is short. It passes by in a blink. Even if the guy's every kind of jerk, he at least deserves a shot at knowing his kid."

I wished I'd never told Howard so much. Edward had made me love him as I'd never loved anyone. He'd filled me with his child. He'd made me so happy.

But he hadn't wanted me. He hadn't wanted any of it. Love. Children. Happiness.

Bluebirds soared above my mother's garden, singing as they lifted higher into the cloudless blue sky. Something caught in my throat, and I looked away. "He told me he didn't ever want a child. I was doing him a favor."

"People can change. Sometimes for better than you can imagine. He deserved the chance." He looked at me and said softly, "Your mom would have said the same."

I gave a soft gasp. Bringing Mom into it was punching below the belt.

Not that I actually had a belt anymore. Unthinkingly, I put my hand over my swelling body. It was a good thing that long dresses were in style, because now I was in my third trimester, none of my regular clothes fit me anymore. Not even the stretchiest yoga pants.

"He had his chance." I slowly rose to my feet.

"He threw my love back in my face. I'm not giving him the chance to do it to her."

"He hurt you. I get it." My stepfather's rheumy eyes met mine in the bright, unrelenting California sunshine. "But take advice from an old man who loves you. Grab your chance at love when you can. Because right now, you think there will be endless chances." His throat caught. "There won't. You used to know that, until he turned you hard and cynical. When I think of the sweet kid you were, I'd like to punch Edward St. Cyr in the jaw." His bushy gray eyebrows lowered ferociously. "If I ever meet him—"

The hinge of the garden gate squeaked. I looked up. "Jason—"

But it wasn't Jason. Looking across the dappled sunlight of the garden, my heart was suddenly in my throat.

Edward stood across the green grass, in front of the bright pink flowers. Sunlight illuminated his dark hair, and luminous, deep blue eyes.

"Is it true?" He lowered his gaze to my pregnant belly. "You're pregnant?"

My breath caught.

Edward took a step toward me, and another. His

eyes devoured me, as if he'd been dreaming of me for months and could hardly believe I wasn't a dream now.

"Is it mine?" he said quietly. "Or Jason Black's?"

I trembled, my hands shaking.

"Yours," Howard said helpfully.

I turned on him in outrage. "Howard!"

"Oh, c'mon." He rolled his eyes. "It's not as if you were going to lie. At least not for long," he amended, looking at me more closely.

"You're meddling," I accused.

"I'm saving you some trouble. You can thank me later. Excuse me." My stepfather walked toward the garden gate. He stopped in front of Edward. "About time you showed up." He rubbed his jowly chin thoughtfully. "I actually owe you a punch in the jaw—"

"Howard!" I cried.

"Later," he said hastily, glancing back at me, and he let himself out the gate. Leaving us alone.

Edward and I stared at each other across the soft green grass. He had a five-o'clock shadow on the hard edge of his jawline, and shadows beneath his eyes, as if he hadn't slept in days. And he'd never looked so beautiful to me. Never, ever.

Except I didn't care about him anymore. I didn't.

And I wouldn't. I took a deep breath. "What are you doing here?"

"I'm here…" Edward seemed uncharacteristically uncertain. His gaze lowered to my belly, the shape of which was clearly visible beneath my cotton maxi dress. "I saw a picture of you online. The article said Jason Black was your boyfriend but…"

"I'm due in September."

He did the math quickly in his head, then his lips twisted downward. "So I'm the father."

I looked down at the grass, the color of emeralds, lush and spikey. "Sorry. Yes."

He shook his head. "How is it possible? We were so careful—"

"Not careful enough, apparently."

"You knew you were pregnant when you left London, didn't you?" His voice was deceptively quiet. "You knew, and you didn't tell me."

"I did you a favor."

"A favor?"

"You didn't want a child. You were very clear." My teeth chattered with emotion. I wrapped my arms around my body, which was suddenly shivering in the bright July sunlight. "You didn't want a child, and you didn't want me."

He came closer to me. "So you took your revenge?"

I shook my head fiercely. "I wanted to tell you about the baby. I tried! But the moment I told you I loved you, you ran out of the house in terror!"

He gritted his teeth. "Don't you *dare* try to—"

"You said you wanted a clean break!" In spite of my best efforts to stay calm, my voice was shrill. "You said you never wanted to see me again! I tried to tell you, but you ran out of the house rather than listen to me! Don't you remember?"

Edward sucked in his breath. Then he came closer in the dappled sunlight, until he stood inches away from me. "Is that why you turned to Jason—because I wouldn't listen?" He moved closer. "Or was he the one you really wanted all along?"

"I wanted you." My voice was flat. "I told you. I was in love with you. I loved you as I'll never love anyone again."

He blinked.

"Loved."

"Past tense." I shook my head. "Loving you nearly killed me. You rejected me. Abandoned me," I whispered. "I couldn't bear for you to reject her, too."

He exhaled, as if he were breathing toxic fumes. Then his eyes flew open. "*Her?*"

I nodded. "I'm having a little girl."

His face filled with wonder and he reached towards me. "We're having a girl...."

I jerked back before he could touch me. "*We're* not. I am. I can support us now." My eyes hardened. "We don't need you."

Pain flashed across his handsome face, then the lines of his cheekbones and dark jawline tightened. "You're not even giving me a chance."

"I tried that already."

He gritted his teeth. "I didn't know you were pregnant."

"You told me straight out you never wanted a child. Never. Never ever."

"People can change."

"What are you trying to say, Edward?" I clenched my hands at my sides. "Are you saying now I don't need you, now I don't even *want* you, you suddenly want to be part of our lives?" I tossed my head. "Forget it!"

His expression hardened. "Because you now have what you really wanted all along—an acting career, and Jason Black?"

"Leave him out of this!"

He set his jaw. "Has he asked you to marry him?"

I looked away.

"He has, hasn't he?" Edward's voice hit me like a blow. "So you could forgive him for sleeping with your stepsister? But not me for letting you go?"

"Look," I said acidly, glaring at him. "I don't know what kind of spiritual breakdown you're going through—seems a little early for a midlife crisis, isn't it? But keep us out of it."

"She's my daughter."

"Just biologically."

"*Just?*" he said incredulously.

"You can't be responsible for a houseplant. You said so yourself!"

"I could change."

"Don't."

My single cold word hung in the air between us. He took a deep breath, looking down at me.

"What happened to you, Diana?" he said softly.

I lifted my head. "Don't you know? Can't you tell? The naive woman you knew died in London."

"Oh my God…" he whispered, reaching towards me. Wild-eyed, I backed away. He straightened, setting down his hands at his sides. "All right, Diana," he said quietly. "All right."

Blinking fast, willing myself not to cry, I walked away from him. My knees felt weak. I sank into a marble bench hidden amid a cool, shadowy copse of trees. But he followed, standing a few yards away.

I looked at him in the sunshine, in front of the brilliant colors of my mother's roses.

"You were right all along," I said. "I should have listened to you when you tried to tell me. Love is a suckers' game." I looked away. "The only way to win is not to play."

He took a single staggering step back from me. Then, with a deep breath, he held himself still. As if he were trying to hold himself back from— from what?

Clenching his hands at his sides, Edward came and sat beside me, on the other end of the bench, careful not to touch me.

"I'm sorry," he said quietly. "I never wanted you to learn that from me."

"You helped me out. Made me grow up."

"Let me tell you something else now." Sunlight brushed his dark blue eyes, and I saw the depths, like a brilliant sparkling light illuminating the deepest, darkest ocean. "I never should have let you go."

My lips parted. I stared up at him in shock.

He gave me a sudden crooked smile. "From the moment you left, I knew I'd made the greatest mistake of my life. In fact," he said in a low voice, "it was no life at all." He leaned forward. "I came to California to try to win you back."

I stared at him, stricken.

I could hardly believe Edward was sitting in my mother's garden in Beverly Hills. Sitting beside me on the marble bench Howard had given her one year for Mother's Day.

"You want me back?" I breathed.

He nodded. "More than anything."

We all create our own garden, Mom used to say. Gardening was a lot like life, in her opinion. Sure, plants depended on sun and soil, but the most important thing was the gardener. What choices did she make? Did she hack off roses with a dull blade? Did she overwater the ivy? Did she let wisteria grow wild, until it overran the walls, blocking all light in an insurmountable thicket of twisted vine? The garden you had showed the choices you'd made. What you'd done with the hand nature dealt you.

Now, Edward was offering me a choice I never imagined I'd have. He wanted me back?

I thought of the months of anguish I'd endured after London. He'd nearly destroyed me. I couldn't live through another broken heart. I couldn't.

My shoulders tightened. No. I lifted my chin. I'd finally stopped loving him. It was going to stay that way.

"We all make choices we have to live with," I said quietly. My eyes glittered as I looked at him. "I've moved on. So should you."

"Have you?" He straightened on the bench. And his jaw tightened. "You seem to forget one thing. I'm the baby's father. I have rights."

I stiffened. He was threatening me now?

"So it's like that, is it?"

He took a deep breath. "I don't want to fight you, Diana. It's the last thing I want. I came here to tell you I was wrong."

"Funny." Turning away, I gave a hard laugh. "Because I've decided you were right, ending our affair like you did. A long-term relationship just brings pain. Friends with benefits—that's the only way to go."

"Is that what you have with Jason?" he said roughly.

I shrugged. "More or less."

"Well, which is it? More—or less?"

"More friendship, less benefits."

"How much less?"

Gritting my teeth, I grudgingly admitted, "None."

He relaxed slightly. He leaned forward. "Diana, don't you want our child to have what you had—two parents? A real home?"

"Sure." I shrugged. "In a perfect world…"

"She can have it. All you have to do is say yes."

I lifted my chin. "What are you asking me, exactly?"

"I'm asking you, you little fool," his eyes glittered, "to marry me."

I was dreaming. I sat in shock beside him on the cool marble bench. Above the palm trees, I heard the birds singing as they crossed the blue sky. A soft summer wind blew through the flowers, causing the scent of roses to waft over me like an embrace. The only sound was the bluebirds, and a hummingbird and the lazy buzzing of the bees in the dappled sunlight.

"What did you say?" I whispered.

Edward stared down at me, his dark eyes intense. "I want to marry you."

I drew back.

"I don't understand." I put a hand to my head, feeling dizzy. "Everything you said in London—you swore you'd never want a wife or child—"

"It's all changed."

"Why?"

"You're pregnant with my child." He looked at me. "And I want you, Diana. I've never stopped wanting you. From the moment you left, I've hungered only for you."

I gave an awkward laugh. "You've had other lovers...."

"No."

My jaw dropped. "It's been four months!"

"I only want you," he said simply.

My heart was pounding. I tried desperately to bring it under control. "You didn't come to California because you wanted me." I lifted my chin. "You only came when you found out I was pregnant."

He clawed back his hair. "I was waiting for you to call me. I thought you would."

I looked at him in disbelief. "You thought I would call you—after what you said to me?"

"Women always try to win me back." A rueful smile curved his lips. "But not you."

I took a deep breath, remembering what it had cost me. I'd felt so alone and heartsick when I'd returned to California. For weeks, I'd cried my-self to sleep—then was tormented in dreams, as hot memories of our nights together forced them-selves upon me when I was sleeping and helpless to fight them.

"Your pregnancy just gave me the reason to come find you. It forced me to do what I'd been afraid to do. To ask you," he said, lifting his gaze to mine, "to come back to me."

Against my will, a shiver rose from deep in-side me. A shiver deeper than fury and stronger than pride.

I stubbornly shook my head.

"I want you," Edward said, his handsome face intent on mine, making me tremble with sensual memories. His gaze fell to my lips. "I need you, Diana."

"Just missing sex..." My voice came out a croak. I cleared my throat. "That isn't a good enough reason to marry someone."

"I don't want to marry you for sex." He sat up straight on the park bench, and I was reminded of how powerful his body was, how much larger than mine. "I want us to be wed. So our child can have a childhood like yours. Not a childhood like mine."

I swallowed, remembering his loneliness then, how his mother had abandoned him when he was ten, and his father had ignored him, except when he could be used as a weapon against his ex-wife. Even the beloved gardener who'd taught him to fish had abruptly left. Boarding school at twelve. A horrible cousin. An empty castle. With only a paid housekeeper to care. That was Edward's childhood.

"You don't need to worry." I briefly touched his shoulder. "Our baby will always be safe and loved." I cradled my hands over my belly. "I promise you."

"I know." His eyes met mine. "Because I'll be there."

I glared at him. "Edward—"

Reaching out, he deliberately put his larger hand over mine, gently on the swell of my belly. I gasped when I felt him touch my hand for the first time, felt the weight of it resting protectively over the child we'd created. "I'm not going to let her go."

He looked at my belly with a trace of a smile on his lips. Then he looked up at me. "Or you."

My mouth went dry.

"But I don't love you," I choked out, as if those magic words were a talisman that could make him disappear. "I'll never love you again."

The words seemed suspended in the air between us. Then he smiled. Moving closer to me, he cupped my cheek.

"Friends with benefits, then."

"And marriage?"

"And definitely that."

"I won't let you do this," I said, trembling beneath his touch. His fingertips stroked softly down my cheek, tracing my full lower lip. My breasts, now lush and full with pregnancy, felt heavy, my nipples hard and aching. I breathed, "You can't just come back, after the way you broke my heart, and force yourself into my life!"

"You mean I have to earn it."

"Well—yes—what are you smiling about?"

"Nothing." He lifted his chin. "I'm not afraid. I know exactly what to do."

"You do?"

"Yes." He slid down the bench until he was right against me. I felt him close to me, so close, and I shivered with heat in the cool shade of the garden. "I'll do whatever it takes to earn back what I've lost."

"You can't." I swallowed. "Yes, you're my baby's father. There's nothing I can do about that. But that's all. I'll never open my heart—or my body—to you again. I won't be your friend. I won't sleep with you. And I definitely won't marry you."

He pulled me into his arms. "We'll see...."

My heart beat fast as he held me against the warmth of his body. I heard the intake of his breath, and realized he was trembling, too. That was my last thought before he turned me to face him. And he lowered his mouth to mine.

He kissed me hungrily, and when his lips touched mine, in spite of my cold anger, I could not fight it. When he kissed me, the colors of the garden whirled around us, pink bougainvillea and green leaves and palm leaves glowing with sun, flying wild into the sky. And against my will, I kissed him back.

Just a kiss. One last kiss of farewell, I told myself. Before I sent him away forever.

CHAPTER SEVEN

THE COOL OCEAN BREEZE came in through open sliding glass doors on the other side of the cottage, oscillating white translucent curtains as I peeked inside the front door.

"Edward?" I called hesitantly, stepping inside the tiny house he had rented on Malibu Beach. "Are you in here?"

No answer. It took several seconds for my eyes to adjust to the light. The old grandfather clock on the other side of the floral sofa said nine o'clock. The tiny galley kitchen was empty and dark.

Edward had asked me so particularly to come over tonight, as soon as I was done filming a commercial on the other side of town. Where was he? Surely he couldn't have forgotten?

For the past month, since he'd arrived in California, he'd gone out of his way to take care of me, putting me first in anything. The only thing he'd flatly refused was to stay away from me.

"Give me a chance to change your mind about me," he said.

I'd told myself it didn't matter. He could pursue me as much as he wanted. I wasn't going to marry him. And after that first amazing kiss in the garden, I stuck to my vow and never let him kiss me again. I think I was afraid what would happen if I did.

The time we'd spent together over the past month had been almost like Cornwall again—only far sunnier, of course, with summery blue skies and bright blue Pacific. And no sex. That was a big change. But that didn't stop Edward from spending every moment with me, taking me out for dinner, giving me foot rubs, helping me shop for baby gear. I continued to sleep in my childhood bedroom at my stepfather's house. One night, when I'd moaned about my cravings for watermelon and caramel pretzel ice cream, he'd showed up at the house with groceries. He'd had to throw a pebble against my window. Because it was three in the morning.

No man was this good. No man could work this hard for long. I couldn't let myself fall for it, because there was no way it would last.

He'd made it clear what he wanted. Marriage. A shared home for our daughter. And me. In his bed.

But it wouldn't last. Soon, his emotional breakdown—or whatever it was—would clear up, and he'd rush back to his selfish playboy workaholic life. As long as I never forgot that, or let down my guard, I told myself I'd be fine. But still…

"When are you going back to London?" I'd demanded yesterday. "How is St. Cyr Global managing without their CEO?"

Edward gave me a crooked grin. "They'll just have to cope."

He'd started accompanying me to OB-GYN visits. When he saw the first ultrasound images of our daughter, and heard her heartbeat, his eyes glistened suspiciously.

"Were those tears?" I asked as we left.

"Don't be ridiculous," he said gruffly, wiping his eyes with the back of his hand. "Dust in my eyes." And to change the subject he offered to take me to dinner at a famous restaurant which cost around four hundred dollars a plate.

I shook my head. "Nah. I want a burger, fries, frozen yogurt. How about a beachside café?"

He smiled at me. "Sure."

"You don't mind?" I asked later, as we sat on a casual wooden patio in Malibu, overlooking parked expensive motorcycles, the Pacific Coast Highway and the wide ocean beyond.

"Nope." Edward shook his head, smiling as he helped himself to one of my fries. "If you're happy, I'm happy."

For the past month, his only apparent job in California had been to take care of me. He treated me as if I were not only the mother of his child, and object of all his desire, but was in fact Queen of the World.

It was pretty hard to resist. In spite of my best efforts, he was slowly wearing me down. I found myself spending every minute with him that I wasn't working.

It irritated Jason to no end. "You never have time for me anymore," he grumbled when we ran into each other last week on a studio lot. "You're falling for him again."

"I'm not," I protested.

But now, I felt so oddly bereft as I walked through Edward's dark, empty beach cottage, I wasn't so sure.

Could he have suddenly decided he was bored

with me and the baby, and flown off to London in his private jet, forgetting that he'd begged me to come over tonight?

Remembering the glow in his eyes as we'd had breakfast that morning, waffles and strawberries at an old diner near the set where I'd filmed a commercial today, I couldn't quite believe it. A low curse lifted to my lips.

Jason was right.

I was starting to trust Edward again.

Starting to let myself care.

Setting my jaw, I walked across the cottage and pushed past the white translucent curtains to the pool area in the back, with its view of the beach. "Edward?"

No answer. For a moment, I closed my eyes, relishing the cool ocean breeze against my overheated skin. It was August now, and the weather was hot, and at my advanced stage of pregnancy, so was I. As I turned back to go inside, my belly jutted so far ahead of me it seemed to be in its own time zone. Sliding the screen door closed behind me, I crossed the living room, my flip-flops thwacking softly against the hardwood floor.

I should have been here hours ago. But the shoot

had gone over, and then I'd gotten a call from my agent on the way here. He'd had news so momentous I'd had to pull over my car.

"This is your big break, Diana," my agent had almost shouted. "You just got offered the girlfriend role in the biggest summer blockbuster. It'll make your career. Another actress fell through at the last minute, and she suggested you…"

"Who suggested me?" I'd said, confused.

"Someone with good taste, that's who. Movie will start shooting a few weeks after your due date," he said, cackling with glee. "How's that for perfect timing? You'll have three whole weeks to lose the baby weight before you need to report to Romania…that won't be a problem, will it, kiddo?"

Lose thirty pounds in three weeks? "Um…" Then I was distracted by the other thing he'd said. "Romania?"

"For three months. Romania is lovely in the fall."

I was dumbfounded. "But I'll have a newborn."

"So? Bring the baby with you. You'll have a nice trailer. Get a nanny." When I didn't answer, he said hastily, "Or leave the kid here with its dad. Whatever you want. But you can't turn this role down, Diana. Don't you get it? It's a starring role. Your name will be above the title. This is your big chance."

"Yeah," I'd said, wondering why I didn't feel more thrilled. Of course I would say yes. I had no choice. Wasn't this what I'd wanted, what I'd dreamed of and strived for? This kind of luck didn't happen every day. But as I imagined losing thirty pounds in three weeks then taking my newborn off to live in a Romanian trailer, all I felt was exhausted. "I…have to think about it."

"Are you kidding?" He'd been stunned. "If you'd turn this down, I'm not sure how much I can help you in the future," he'd said warningly. "I need to feel like we're on the same team."

"I understand."

"I'll call you for your answer first thing tomorrow. Make it the right one."

I didn't know what to do. I was tempted to talk it over with Edward, but I had the feeling he'd just tell me he supported whatever I wanted to do. Heck, for all I knew, he'd come to Romania with me. So much had changed.

So where was Edward now? I was two hours late. Had he given up waiting for me and left, to walk off his irritation with a stroll on the beach?

Malibu was a beautiful place. I should know. I was the one who'd talked him into renting this place.

The very first day he'd come to Beverly Hills, he'd recklessly told me he planned to buy a nearby house, on sale for twenty million dollars. "I want to be close to you." Privately, I'd thought he was out of his mind; even more privately, I thought if he lived forty minutes away, it would be a case of *out of sight, out of mind* and he'd stop pursuing me. So I'd convinced him he should instead rent a beach house getaway.

"You have to help me pick out the house," Edward had agreed. Backed into a corner, I'd consented. The estate agent had taken us to ritzy McMansions all over town, but I hadn't loved any of the newly built palaces, all of them the same with their seven bedrooms and ten bathrooms, with their tennis courts and home theaters and wine cellars. When Edward saw I wasn't interested in them, he wasn't either. Finally, in an act of pure desperation, the estate agent had brought us here.

Built in the 1940s on Malibu Beach, this cottage was squat and ugly compared to the three-story glass mansions around it. When Edward saw it, he almost told her to drive on.

"Wait," I'd said, putting my hand on his arm. Something about the tiny, rickety house had reminded me of my family home in Pasadena, where I'd lived when I was a very young child, before my father had died.

When he saw my face, Edward was suddenly willing to overlook the house's flaws. Good thing, because there were so many. No air conditioning. The kitchen was ridiculously tiny and last remodeled in 1972. The wooden floorboards creaked, the dust was thick and the furniture was covered with white sheets. When I pulled the sheet off the baby grand piano, a dust cloud kicked up and made us all cough, even the estate agent.

"I shouldn't have brought you here," she said apologetically.

"No," I'd whispered. "I love it."

"We'll take it," Edward said.

But where was he now? I went heavily up the creaking stairs to the second floor. I'd been up here only once before, when we'd toured the house with the estate agent. It was just a small attic bedroom with slanted ceilings, and a tiny balcony overlooking the ocean.

As I reached the top of the stairs, the bedroom was in shadow. I saw only the brilliant slash of orange and persimmon to the west as the red ball of the sun fell like fire into the sea.

Then I saw Edward, sitting on the bed.

And then…

I sucked in my breath.

Hundreds of rose petals in a multitude of colors had been scattered across the bed and floor, illuminated by tapered white candles on the nightstands and handmade shelves. When Edward saw me standing in the doorway, in my sundress and casual ponytail, he rose from the bed. His chest and feet were bare. He wore only snug jeans that showed off his tanned skin, and the shape of his well-muscled legs. Stepping toward me, he smiled.

"I've been waiting for you."

"I can see that," I whispered, knowing I was in trouble. Knowing I should *run*.

He lifted a long-stemmed red rose from a nearby vase. Leaning forward, he stroked the softest part of the rose against my cheek. "I know your secret."

I blinked. "My…my secret?"

Leaning back, he gave me a lazily sensual smile. "How you tried to resist me. And failed."

"I haven't. I haven't agreed to marriage or fallen into bed with you. Not yet," I choked out. Then blushed when I realized the insinuation was that I soon would.

His smile lifted to a grin. He nodded toward a pile of books in a box in a corner of the room. "I just got that box this afternoon from Mrs. Mac-Whirter. It seems you left something, buried in your bedroom closet at Penryth Hall."

I looked down at the open box. Sitting on top was the faded dust jacket of the fine manual written by Mrs. Warreldy-Gribbley, *Private Nursing: How to Care for a Patient in His Home Whilst Maintaining Professional Distance and Avoiding Immoral Advances from Your Employer.*

"Oh," I said lamely, looking back at Edward with my cheeks on fire.

He gave a low laugh. "Didn't do you much good, did it?"

Biting my lip, I shook my head.

Tilting his head, he looked at me wickedly. "What do you think Mrs. Warreldy-Gribbley would say if she saw you now?"

I looked down at my hugely pregnant belly,

which strained the knit fabric of my sundress. "I'm not sure she'd have the words."

"I think…" He ran his fingertips lightly over my bare shoulder, turning me to face him. "She'd tell you to marry me."

A tremble went through my body. My bare shoulder pulsed heat from the place when he touched me.

Scowling, I glared at him. "Do you always get your own way?"

Lifting his hand, he cupped my cheek.

"Ask me tomorrow," he said softly.

And Edward fell to one knee before me.

I stared down at him, my mouth wide with shock. "What are you doing?"

"What I should have done long ago." He looked up at me in the small, shadowy attic bedroom. "You know I want to marry you, Diana. I'm asking you one last time. With everything I've got," he said quietly. "All I want is to make you happy." He drew a black velvet box from his jeans pocket and held it up in the flickering candlelight. "Will you give me the chance?"

Looking down at him, I couldn't move or breathe. I suddenly knew that whatever happiness or misery came to me—and my daughter—would all stem from the choice I made in this moment.

"Diana…" Edward opened the black velvet box. "Will you marry me?"

I saw the enormous diamond ring and covered my mouth with my hands. I blinked hard, unable to believe my eyes. "Is that thing real?" I breathed. "It's the size of an iceberg—"

"You deserve the best," he said quietly.

I'd spent years in Hollywood. So I'd seen big diamonds before. Madison had worn lots of big diamonds to awards shows—gorgeous borrowed jewels to go with her gorgeous borrowed gowns. But even in Hollywood, the million-dollar jewelry was an illusion. When the event was over, the jewelry had to be returned. Faster than you can say *glass slipper.*

But this wasn't borrowed. This was meant to last.

Edward meant this to last.

"Don't do this to me," I whispered, stricken. "We don't need to get married. We can live apart, but still raise her together…."

"That's not what I want," he said quietly, still on one knee. "What is your answer?"

I looked down at him. Looked at the rose petals, the candlelight. I took a deep breath. "You'll change your mind...."

"I won't." He hesitated. "But if you love someone else..."

I shook my head.

"Then what?" he asked gently.

I took a deep breath, and met his eyes.

"I'm scared. I loved you once, and it nearly destroyed me."

His hand seemed to tighten on the black velvet box. His voice was low. "You don't have to love me."

Marriage without love? The thought was a jarring one. I licked my lips. "I'm afraid if I say yes, you'll soon regret it. You'll wish you could be single again, and date all those women...."

"I'll only regret it," he said, "if you say no."

"Where would we live?" A hysterical laugh bubbled to my lips. "You don't want to spend your life waiting for me, as I film commercials... Sooner or later you'll have to get back to work."

He looked up at me, his dark eyes inscrutable in the fading twilight. "You're right."

"I won't live in London. We were so unhappy there. Both of us."

"There are other choices," he said quietly.

"Like what?"

"The whole world." Rising to his feet, he pulled my left hand against his chest, over his heart. "Just let me give it to you."

I could feel his heart pounding beneath my hand. The strong rapid beat matched my own. My fingers curled against his warm skin.

"I won't let you break my heart again," I choked out.

"I'll never hurt you, Diana. Ever." Dropping the rose and the black velvet box to the end table, Edward pulled me into his arms. His hands stroked back my hair, down my bare back that was only covered with the crisscross lines of my sundress. "Let me show you...."

Lowering his head to mine, he kissed me.

And this time, I could not resist.

His lips were tender. They enticed me, lured me, soft and sensual as the whisper of a sigh. I exhaled. There could be no fighting this. It didn't just feel as if he were embracing my body. It felt like he was caressing my soul.

"Marry me, Diana," he whispered, his lips brushing against mine.

All the reasons I couldn't marry him rose to my

mind, but as he kissed me they dissipated into thin air like mist.

What was fear, against the incessant pull of his body against mine? His muscles were solid beneath my hands, his body powerful and strong. Something to cling to. Someone to believe in. And oh, how I wanted to believe.

I'd been keeping the secret for so long. Even from myself. But it had been right there all along. The real secret in my heart.

I loved Edward.

I'd never stopped loving him.

And all I'd ever wanted was for him to love me back.…

"Say yes." Edward kissed my cheeks, my lips, my eyelids. "Say it—"

"Yes," I breathed.

He drew back. His handsome face looked vulnerable, his blue eyes caught between hope and doubt. "Do you mean it?"

Please let this be right. Please let this not be a mistake.

Unable to speak, I nodded.

Grabbing the black velvet box, Edward slid the obscenely huge diamond ring onto the fourth finger of my left hand. I felt its heavy weight for just a moment before he lifted my hand to his lips, kissing my palm.

In the candlelit bedroom, with the open window overlooking the twilight sea, the reverence of his gesture, like a private unspoken vow, lacerated my heart.

"You said yes," he said in wonder. He shook his head. "I was starting to think…"

His voice trailed off. With an intake of breath, he lifted me in his arms, as if I weighed nothing at all. Gently setting me down on his bed, he pulled off my sandals one by one, kissing the tender hollow of each foot.

Leaning forward, he pulled off my sundress, leaving me stretched across the bed in only my white cotton panties and a bra that seemed barely adequate, trapped between my overflowing breasts and full pregnant belly. The enormous diamond ring on my left hand felt heavy as a shackle, making me suddenly afraid. After everything I knew about Edward's soul, was agreeing to marry him, giving him not just body and soul but offering up all my future, all my life, and my child's in the bargain—an act of insanity?

Edward cupped my face in his hands. His expression was tender, his eyes shining. "All I want is to take care of you forever...."

"I want to do the same for you." I was in so deep now. I wanted desperately to believe the fantasy was true. Wrapping my arms around his shoulders, I kissed him with trembling lips. Twining his hands in my hair, he kissed me back, matching my passion, exceeding it. A fire roared through me, and I gasped.

Drawing back, he pulled off his clothes and gently lay me back against the bed. My hair tumbled over the pillows. I shivered, closing my eyes as he kissed down my neck. His lips were warm beneath the cool ocean breeze blowing through the window. I breathed in the scent of him, clean and masculine, with the sea air and the rose petals scattered around us.

He unhooked my bra. I gasped as I felt his lips nuzzle my breast before he drew my full nipple gently into his mouth. Pregnancy had made my breasts so big, he had to hold each with both hands in its turn. I gripped his shoulders tightly.

Pulling back, he looked down at me. "You're in your third trimester," he murmured wickedly. "The doctor said you shouldn't spend too long on your back...."

Before I knew what was happening, he rolled me over, so I was on top of him. He pulled my knees apart, so I straddled his hips. My belly was huge between us, my breasts hanging almost to his face as I leaned forward to kiss him. I felt the size of him, hard and huge between my legs and the pregnancy hormones I'd tried to ignore for months suddenly rocketed uncontrollably through me, leaving me weak with lust. Pulling up, I came down hard, impaling myself, drawing him deep and thick inside me. He gasped, putting his hands on my hips. Not stopping, not waiting, I rocked back and forth, riding him with increasing speed until he was stretching me to the limit, filling me to the core, and with a loud cry, I exploded, and so did he. We both soared amid the fading purple shadows of the night.

Afterward, he drew me close, holding me in his arms. He kissed my sweaty temple. "I never want to let you go."

"So don't," I whispered. My body felt illuminated, glowing with happiness. I pressed my cheek against the warmth of his bare skin, glorying in the feel of his arm wrapped snugly around me in bed.

"Let's go to Las Vegas," he said suddenly.

Blinking, I lifted my head to look at him. "You want to elope?"

I thought I saw a shadow cross his eyes. Then he gave me a lazy smile. "I don't want to give you the chance to change your mind."

"I won't." I looked down at my engagement ring. "Though this thing is so heavy, I feel lop-sided. What is it, ten carats?"

He grinned. "Twenty."

"What! I think you might have overdone it!"

"I'll get you a ring for your other hand. Then it won't be a problem." He stroked my cheek. "Just say you'll run away with me tomorrow."

It sounded like a dream. But...I bit my lip. "Without my family?"

He gave a low laugh. "I should have known you wouldn't like that thought. Bring Howard with us, then. And whomever else you want. Plenty of room on the jet." He stroked his jaw ruefully. "Though I'm still waiting for him to hit me on the jaw."

I snorted. "Howard would never go through with it. He loves you too much now." Then my smile faded. "Madison is coming home tonight...."

"From Mongolia? Is it the first time you've seen her since Penryth Hall?"

"Yeah. I need to try to work things out." I sighed. Rising to my feet, I started to pull on my clothes.

"Don't go." He held out his arm. "Stay with me tonight."

I looked at him longingly, then shook my head. "I need to talk to Madison. But then..." I looked at him. "If she forgives me for breaking up her engagement, and Howard can come, then..."

"Then?" he said, his voice filled with rising hope.

I smiled at him. I felt so happy, there were tears in my eyes. "Then I'll elope with you in the morning."

With an intake of breath, he rose to his feet. Taking me in his arms, he kissed me softly. "Go home. See your family tonight." He gave me a smile that was brighter than the sun. "And I'll see you tomorrow."

It felt so good in his arms, so warm, so right. It felt—like home. I bit my lip, suddenly reluctant to leave. "On second thought, maybe I could stay here tonight. I'll see Madison tomorrow...."

With a low laugh, he shook his head. "No. Go. Talk to them. Then we can start our new lives tomorrow." Drawing back, Edward looked thoughtful. "Anyway, I think there's something else I need to do tonight."

I frowned. "What?"

"Just something," he said evasively.

"Bachelor party?" I half joked. He didn't even crack a smile.

"It's nothing." Turning away, he pulled on his jeans. His face was hidden in shadow. "Just one last thing I want to do before I say my marriage vows."

"Oh?" I stared at him, waiting for him to explain.

He suddenly wouldn't meet my gaze. "I'll walk you out."

A moment later, I backed my car down the small driveway of the Malibu cottage, and soon eased onto the Pacific Coast Highway. As I looked out at the moonlight flickering over the Pacific, in the flashes of flat beach between the tightly packed million-dollar houses clinging to the strip of shore, I'd suddenly felt I'd never been so happy. Or so terrified.

Because I loved him.

He'd never once said he loved me.

I gripped the steering wheel. *It'll be fine,* I told myself. Edward didn't need to love me. We could still be happy together. Friends. Parents. Lovers. Partners.

But what was he so anxious to do tonight, "before we spoke our vows"?

It didn't matter. He'd promised he'd never break my heart again. It couldn't be another woman or anything like that. He was probably just planning a surprise for me. Like a wedding gift. When I saw it in the morning, I'd have a good laugh at my own fears. Getting married should mean that I could trust him. I never needed to feel insecure again. Right?

It's nothing. Just one last thing I want to do before I say my marriage vows.

Oh, this was ridiculous. I was only four blocks away from my stepfather's house in Beverly Hills when I banged on the steering wheel in irritation, then yelped as the big diamond cut sharply into my hand. Sucking my finger, I pulled over.

Forget this. I was going back to Malibu to find out what he was hiding from me. If it was some awesome wedding gift, I'd hate myself later for wrecking the surprise.

I flipped my car around, heading back west, toward Malibu.

Thirty minutes later, I was turning down Edward's small street, when I saw an expensive SUV pull ahead of me. It was going way too fast down the lane. Idiot, I thought. Then to my shock, it pulled haphazardly into Edward's driveway. A woman leapt out of the driver's seat. But not just any woman.

It was Victoria. The beautiful, vicious wife of Edward's cousin, Rupert. Dressed in a tight, sexy red cocktail dress and six-inch high heels.

I forced myself to keep driving slowly, past the cottage without stopping. But in my rearview mirror, I saw the cottage door open. Edward welcomed her swiftly inside.

Then the door closed behind them.

A horn honked ahead of me, and I swerved just in time to avoid crashing into opposing traffic. Cold sweat covered my body. This was what he wanted to do before he spoke marriage vows?

A bachelor party for two?

I remembered Victoria's earlier words: *I wanted him so badly, I would have done anything to get into his bed. Anything.*

Numbly, I turned back on the highway, back toward Los Angeles.

There had to be some rational reason for Victoria to be with Edward tonight. Something beyond the obvious. But as I tried to come up with a reason, all I could think about was that Edward had never claimed to love me. Not in all this time. He'd said he wanted us to marry for the baby's sake. And that he wanted me in his bed.

He hadn't yet promised fidelity. So it wasn't like he'd broken any vows. No. The only promise he'd broken was when he'd said he would never break my heart.

Why was Victoria there, alone with him in the house? Why would she visit him so late at night, wearing a skintight red dress? Why was she even in California at all?

I wiped my eyes savagely.

Traffic was light, late as it was, and I soon pulled past the gate of Howard's white colonial house. I saw Madison's expensive red convertible parked in the driveway. A car as red and wicked and expensive as Victoria St. Cyr's dress as she'd snuck in for a private tête-à-tête with the man I was supposed to marry tomorrow.

My legs trembled as I walked inside the house. Inside the large, lavish kitchen, I saw Howard and Madison sitting at the table, smiling and talking. But in this moment, I couldn't deal with it. I started to walk past the kitchen, but she saw me. She rose to her feet, her face serious.

"Diana," she said quietly. "It's good to see you again."

I stopped, clenching my hands at my sides. Madison looked tanner, a little weathered, her cheeks a little fuller. No makeup. No false eyelashes. Her blond hair was lightened by sun. She was wearing a white cotton T-shirt, jeans and flip-flops.

"You look—different," I said slowly.

"And you look pregnant." She smiled. "Dad told me you and Edward are back together…."

Tears rose to my eyes. "I'm tired," I choked out. "Excuse me. I have to go—to bed…."

I made it to my bedroom just in time, before the sobs started. Even with the air conditioning, the air felt oppressively hot. I stripped down to a tank top and tiny shorts and collapsed on the bed. Posters on the walls that I'd put up as a hopeful teenager, of places I'd hoped to see and the life I'd hoped to live, stared down at me mournfully. It felt like the walls were closing in.

As my head hit the pillow, I wept, covering my

face, wept with choked sobs until there were no tears left, and I slept.

The phone woke me up. I flung my arm to answer it.

"What is your answer?" My agent's voice pleaded.

Slowly, I sat up in bed. My hair felt smashed against the side of my face, and the tank top I'd been sleeping in barely covered my breasts properly. I felt sore, too. For a moment I smiled, remembering how Edward had made love to me last night.

Then I remembered what had happened afterward. How I'd seen Victoria sneaking into his house for one last fling.

It's nothing. Just one last thing I want to do before I say my marriage vows

Cold despair seeped through me, and I pulled up my comforter almost to my neck.

"Well, Diana?" My agent said with desperate good cheer. "Do you want to be a star?"

I felt awful. Outside, the morning light was clear, the sky a pale blue. It almost never rained in California. Not like Cornwall. I missed the fog and bluster and wild gray storms. They suited me better.

"Diana? The blockbuster in Romania? Are you in?"

"Sure," I said dully. "Why not?"

His congratulations were so loud I had to pull the phone away from my ear. Then he started talking about terms and conditions and other contract stuff I didn't care about. Hanging up, I pulled on a robe and went downstairs.

"Rough night?" Madison looked up from the kitchen table, where she was now eating a bowl of cornflakes. Then her eyes widened. "Nice ring."

I looked down at my left hand. "Yeah," I said dully. "Want it?"

She laughed. "Good one. So you're engaged? I'm so happy for—"

"Edward's cheating on me."

Madison's mouth fell open. Then she looked dubious. "Are you sure? He seemed so in love with you last December. I mean, I even flirted with him," she blushed a little, "and he totally froze me out."

"I'm sure. I saw a woman he knows, his cousin's wife, going into his place late last night. Wearing a sexy dress."

"There could be all kinds of reasons for that. Geez. Maybe, um…" She frowned, scratching her head. "Hmm."

"I don't want to talk about it," I said, grabbing the milk and a bowl.

Madison pressed her lips together. "All right," she said finally. "Whatever you need. I'm here for you."

I stared at her incredulously. "What happened to you in Mongolia?"

"What do you mean?"

"You seem so—different."

"I grew up, I guess," she said quietly. "I decided to stop taking other people's stuff. Their careers. Their lovers. It never made me happy. It only made me feel bad about myself." Her eyes met mine as she whispered, "I'm so sorry for what I did to you."

I stared at her in shock, trying not to cry.

Then Madison's mouth fell open as she looked past me. In slow motion, I turned around.

Edward stood in the kitchen doorway behind me, dressed in a tuxedo that was molded to his perfect body. He smiled, looking from Madison to me. "Looks like all is forgiven." His blue eyes glowed with joy. "How soon can you be ready to go?"

My lips parted in a silent gasp. Then snapped shut.

How *dare* he act like this—look at me as if he loved me—when he'd been with another woman last night? And *Victoria,* of all the women on earth! Did he truly have no soul? I couldn't bear to even look him in the face.

Reaching down, I pulled off the enormous diamond ring. My fingers were swollen, so I had to yank hard. I held it out to him coldly.

"I've changed my mind," I said. "I can't marry you."

His broad shoulders seemed to flinch. There was a small sound from the back of his throat. He took a single step forward. I heard his low demand of a single word.

"Why."

He was looking at me as if I'd betrayed him. As if I'd broken his heart. My throat hurt. How could Edward look at me like that, when he was the one who had never loved me?

Lifting my chin, I looked at him, my fists clenched almost violently. "I thought I could marry you without love," I whispered. Shuddering, I shook my head. "I can't." It was tantamount to admitting my own love for him. I felt like a pathetic fool. "I want the real thing."

My arm shook as I continued to hold out the ring.

He stared down at the twenty-carat diamond ring as if it were poison. He seemed to shudder. "Keep it."

"I can't." I pushed the ring into his hands. My heart hurt so much I could hardly keep from crying. "It's better this way. You can go back to London, and I'll be going to Romania to star in a movie...." The movie? Who cared about that? What was I even saying? I shook my head desperately. "We'll work out custody. You can visit our baby whenever you want."

He looked down at the enormous diamond ring, gleaming in his hand.

"Visit?" he said dully.

"Yes, of course, you..." My throat constricted. "I just want you to be free."

"Free." He lifted expressionless eyes to mine.

Unable to speak, I nodded.

"I thought I could make you happy." His voice was like a sigh, the last breath of a dying man.

He tried to smile even as I saw a suspicious sheen in his eyes. "But I can't force you to marry me. Of course you deserve love. You deserve everything."

My heart twisted. I felt as if I were drowning in the haunted sea of his eyes, seeing right through his armor to the anguished soul within. Was it possible I was wrong? Was there any other explanation for what I'd seen?

"What did you do last night?" I cried out.

Staring down at me, he sucked in his breath. Then he grimly shook his head. "It doesn't matter."

"Tell me," I begged. I knew I was making a fool of myself, but I couldn't stop. If there was any chance, any chance at all that I was wrong... "What did you do when I left you last night?"

He stared down at me for a moment in the kitchen. Then he slowly shook his head.

"It's better you don't know," he said quietly. Leaning forward, he cupped my cheek. "I will always provide for you and the baby, Diana." Leaning down, he kissed me softly, one last time. "Take care of her. Be happy."

And he was gone.

I stared after him, gazing at the empty doorway,

standing on the cold tile floor wearing a robe, a tank top that didn't quite cover my belly, skimpy sleep shorts and a dumb expression.

My stepfather's lavish, enormous kitchen turned blurry around me and I realized I was crying. I couldn't even feel the tears. All I could think was that I'd been so stupid. I'd let Edward St. Cyr break my heart not once, but twice....

"You are *so stupid,*" Madison said aloud, as if she'd read my mind and agreed wholeheartedly. Wiping my cheeks, I looked down at her sitting at the table. I'd forgotten she was there.

She was shaking her head in disgust. "You gave him up for a movie? No career can ever fill the place in your heart where love should be." She gave a harsh laugh. "I should know."

"He doesn't love me," I whispered.

"Are you insane?" She looked as if she thought I was. "Did you see the way he looked at you? And from everything Dad told me about how he's been waiting on you hand and foot..." She snorted. "No man does that for a woman, unless he's desperately in love. Especially a man like Edward St. Cyr."

"He doesn't love me," I repeated, but my voice had turned uncertain. "He just said he didn't."

My stepsister looked at me incredulously. "You said you deserved a marriage based on love, and he agreed with you. It sounded like you didn't love *him*."

"What?" I put my hand to my forehead. A tremble was coming up through my body like an earthquake, rising from my feet to my legs to my heart. "Edward knows I love him. He has to know."

"Did you tell him? Recently, I mean?"

"No, I..." I bit my lip. I'd told him in London, before he'd sent me away. But never since then. Desperately, I shook my head. "He doesn't love me. He wanted to marry me for the baby's sake, that's all." I looked down at my huge baby bump. "If he'd loved me..."

I sucked in my breath, covering my mouth with my hand.

If Edward had loved me, he would have devoted himself to me, night and day, waiting for me to finish work, letting me choose restaurants, taking me to the doctor, rubbing my feet. Driving watermelon and ice cream to my house at three in the morning. He would have let me choose the house we'd live in. I would have been more important than his career.

His friends.

His country.

I always imagined love to be an action, not a word. His words in London came back to haunt me. *If I loved someone, I wouldn't say it, I'd show it. I'd take care of her, putting her needs ahead of my own. I'd put my whole soul into making her happy....*

A choked sound came from the back of my throat.

What kind of man would do so much for a woman, unless he loved her?

And worse—what kind of woman would not even notice, until it was too late?

"He loves you," Madison said quietly behind me. "And you threw it away for some stupid role in a movie." Her lips curled as she shook her head. "When I suggested you to the movie producer, I thought I was making amends for *Moxie McSocksie....*"

"You're the one who suggested me for the part?" I breathed.

"Yeah." She looked at me accusingly. "I didn't know you'd use the movie as an excuse to ruin your life!"

"You're one to talk," I said weakly.

"I know." She held her hands wide. "Look at me, Diana. Totally alone. With the hole in my heart. If a man ever loved me like that, if he saw all my flaws and could love me anyway…" She looked away. "I'd never let him go."

"He cheated on me," I whispered.

She lifted an eyebrow. "Are you still so sure?"

I stared at her. Then I turned and ran up to my bedroom. I dug through my purse until I found an old ratty card. My heart pounded as I dialed a number on my phone.

"Hello?" the woman's voice said.

"Victoria," I said desperately. "What were you doing with Edward last night?"

"Who's that?" She paused. "Diana?"

"Why were you at his house? Why are you even in California?"

Victoria laughed. "As if you didn't know. But I'm glad you called. I wanted to thank you. I misjudged you, Diana. You are a wonderful, wonderful person. Rupert and I will never forget…."

I gripped the phone. "*What are you talking about?*"

"The shares." She paused. "Do you really not know?"

"Shares?"

She gave a tinkly laugh. "For weeks, Edward hinted he might sell his shares of St. Cyr Global. Yesterday Rupert finally had to go back to London, but I stayed here with the children. Edward suddenly called my mobile last night, while I was at a friend's party in Santa Monica. I rushed over to sign the contract, before he could change his mind!"

Whatever I'd expected, that hadn't been it.

"What?"

"Oh, dear. Have I let the cat out of the bag? Edward did say he was doing it as a sort of wedding present, to both of you. New life, new career, all that. I gather you're eloping? Let me know where you're registered and I'll send something. We owe you. I promise you're leaving the company in good hands. And Diana?"

"Yes?" I repeated, my voice a gaspy wheeze.

"Welcome to the family!" she said heartily, and hung up.

My legs trembled. I slowly walked down the stairs, feeling like an old woman. Grief and heartache were building inside me, going radioactive, making my body weak, destroying me cell by cell.

"What?" Madison demanded when I stumbled into the kitchen.

"Edward sold all his shares in his family's company," I choked out. "That was why Victoria was there. That was Edward's big secret. He knew how miserable I was in London. This was his surprise." My throat caught. "It really was a wedding present."

"That's good—isn't it?"

I slowly turned to face her.

"He should have told me," I whispered.

Madison put her arm over my shoulders, as she'd done when we were kids. "He didn't want you to feel guilty."

Guilty? Edward had just sold his birthright for my sake. He could have manipulated me, pointed out everything he'd sacrificed for me. Instead, he'd set me free. Even though I saw now it was the last thing he'd wanted to do. What did it mean?

I wrapped my arms around my body, trying to stop my ice-cold limbs from shaking.

It meant Edward loved me.

"He loves me," I whispered, and I burst into tears. Awful sobs racked my body, almost doubling me over. My stepsister hugged me close.

"It'll be all right," she murmured.

I shook my head. I'd been so determined to never feel heartbreak again, that I'd raced for the exit at the very first scare. Instead of forcing him to tell me the truth about Victoria, I'd thrown his ring back in his face. I thought pride made me do it. It wasn't pride.

It was fear.

"What are you going to do?" Madison said.

I looked up, my heart pounding.

You only have one life, sweetheart, my mom said before she died. *And it goes faster than you ever imagine. So make it count. Be brave. Follow your heart.*

I took a deep breath. "I'm going to be brave," I whispered. "And follow my heart."

Madison's face lifted in a smile. "That's what I was hoping you'd say." Reaching into the pocket of her cutoffs, she tossed me her keys. "Take my car." Her smile turned to a grin. "It's faster."

CHAPTER EIGHT

THE SKY WAS sunny and blue, the air languorous with the scent of lilacs and roses.

Pushing my sunglasses up the bridge of my nose, I clutched my purse and ran toward Madison's red convertible, sandals flapping hard against the driveway, my sundress flying.

I'd tried to call Edward's phone, but there'd been no answer. I'd called the line at the Malibu cottage but there'd been no answer there, either. Why would Edward stay in California now? He wouldn't. Then I'd suddenly had a sick feeling.

I have a private island in the Caribbean. That's where I'd go if I needed to escape a broken heart.... No one can get at you there, Diana. There's no internet, no phones, no way to even get on the island except by my plane.

I'd wanted to run out of the house in my robe and sleeping shorts. Madison had talked me into getting dressed first, in the closest clean thing that still fit me. Twisting my hair into a knot, I jumped into the sports car and drove down the road like a race car driver.

Now, as I drove west toward the coast, the low-lying mist was growing thicker, the air cooler near the ocean. The wind felt fresh and cold against my skin as it blew over the convertible, pulling my hair out of the knot and flying it around me. I pressed on the gas.

I had to reach Edward in time. I had to. Because if his plane took off, I feared it would be a long time before I saw him again....

Red lights glimmered on the cars ahead of me on the highway, forcing me to push on my brakes.

"Come on, come on," I begged aloud, but the cars ahead just grew slower and slower until they stopped altogether. Was there an accident ahead? Someone filming a movie? A visiting political dignitary? Or was it just fate pulling Edward away from me, just when I'd finally realized what I'd lose?

What was the point in having a fast car just to be stopped in L.A. traffic?

I thought I could make you happy. But I can't force you to marry me. Of course you deserve love. You deserve everything.

Every time Edward had loved anyone, they'd

abandoned him. His mother. His father. The woman in Spain. He'd learned not to trust. He'd learned words were cheap. So he'd tried to show me he loved me, in a way more real than words.

How had he found the courage to come to California and humbly tell me he wanted me back? What had it cost him, to try to earn back my love?

Everything, I realized. His heart. His pride. Even his birthright.

All of that—and he'd still let me make the decision. He'd loved me enough to let me go.

Traffic finally picked up speed again. The sun was growing warmer, but I still felt cold, my teeth chattering as I finally arrived at the small nonpublic airport where Edward kept his private jet. He'd been here a month, I realized, and he hadn't used it once. He'd been too busy taking care of me.

Would I be in time?

Driving past the gate, I parked the car helter-skelter in the tiny parking lot, leaving the convertible door open as I ran into the hangar.

No one was there, except for a lone airplane technician looking into the engine of a small Cessna. He straightened. "Can I help you?"

On the other side of the hangar, I heard a loud

engine. Through the open garage door, I saw a jet that looked like Edward's accelerating away, headed down the small landing strip.

"Whose plane is that?" I begged.

The mechanic tilted back his baseball cap. "Well now, I'm not rightly allowed to say…."

"Edward St. Cyr," I choked out. "It's his plane, isn't it? Is he headed to the Caribbean?"

The man frowned. "How the heck did you…"

But I was no longer listening. I took off running, as fast as a heavily pregnant woman could run, across the hangar, straight through the garage door and out onto the tarmac.

"Wait!" I screamed, waving my arms wildly as I ran down the runway, following the plane, trying to catch it though I knew I had no hope. "Edward! Wait!"

The roar of the engine and wind from the propellers swallowed my words, whirling the air around me, pushing me back, making me cough. I felt a sudden pain in my belly and hunched over, at the same moment that the mechanic caught up with me.

"Are you crazy?"

"Edward!" I cried helplessly.

"Are you trying to get yourself killed? Get off

the runway!" The man, who must have thought I was having some kind of pregnancy-related breakdown, half pulled, half carried me back to the hangar. Winded and weak and grief-stricken, I let him.

Edward was gone. I'd lost him forever, because I'd been too much of a coward to fight for him, believe in him, when it counted. I'd let him believe that he could never earn my love, no matter how hard he tried....

Choking out a sob, I covered my face with my hands.

"I love you," I whispered brokenly, sinking to the concrete floor as I said the words I'd been too scared to say to his face. "I love you, Edward...."

"Diana?"

Hardly daring to believe, I looked up.

Edward stood outside the open garage door. Bright California sunshine burnished his dark hair. His face was in shadow, his posture uncertain. He'd changed from his tuxedo to a T-shirt and jeans, and his hands were in his pockets.

On the airstrip behind him, I saw his jet, with the propellers still slowing down. The engine was loud, a blast of white noise. Was he a miracle? A dream? I wiped my eyes, but he was still there.

"You came back…." I gasped. Rising to my feet, I stumbled across the hangar.

"I saw you," he breathed, his eyes hungry on mine. "And I was crazy enough to hope…."

Hiccupping a sob, I threw my arms around his shoulders. "You came back!"

"Of course I did." He held me close, caressing my back. I felt the warmth and strength of his body, smelled the woodsy scent of his cologne. He touched my cheek with a fingertip and said in a voice so tender and raw it twisted my heart, "But you're crying."

Taking his hand in my own, I pressed it against my cheek, looking up at him with eyes swimming in tears. "I thought I'd lost you."

I could feel him tremble. Then he exhaled.

"It's all right, Diana," he said quietly. "You can tell me the truth. If you're trying to be loyal to me for our baby's sake…"

"No!"

"I need you to be happy." He looked away, dropping his hand to his side. "I told myself I could marry you even if you didn't love me. That I could earn you back, and make you love and trust me again, over time."

"Edward…"

"But I can't be the man who takes away the light that's inside you. I can't. I can't condemn you to being my wife when you don't love me. When you might love someone else." Looking away, his jaw tightened as he said, in a voice almost too low for me to hear, "I love you too much for that."

"You love me," I breathed.

Edward gave a low, choked laugh. "And for the first time in my life I know what that means." He looked down at me. "I would do anything for you, Diana. Anything."

"Even sell your shares of St. Cyr Global to your cousin."

He looked started. "How did you know?"

"I called Victoria."

"Why?— How?"

"I saw her going into your house last night."

"You did?"

I hung my head. "You were acting so weird and secretive. I went back to ask you what was going on. Then I saw her going into your house so late, wearing that dress, and I thought the two of you…"

"What!" He blinked in astonishment. "You thought me and *Victoria*…"

"I was so scared of getting hurt again," I whispered, feeling ashamed, "I took the first excuse to run. I'm sorry."

His expression darkened. "When I think of how I treated you in London, I don't blame you." He stroked my cheek. "I didn't want you to feel guilty, or feel like you were under obligation, because I'd made some kind of sacrifice.... Because you were right. I hated that job. I hated the man it made me. Now I'm free." He gave me a sudden grin. "In fact, there's nothing to stop me from coming with you to Romania, as I'm currently unemployed...."

Reaching up, I put my hands over his. "I don't want to go."

He frowned. "What?"

"I thought being an actress was my big dream. But I never wanted to audition." The corners of my mouth quirked. "There was a reason. Whatever my brain tried to tell me I wanted, my heart stubbornly knew it wanted something else entirely."

He pulled me closer, running his hands over my face, my hair, my back. "What?"

I thought of my mother, and the life she'd lived. Hannah Maywood Lowe had never been famous or celebrated. People who didn't know her would have thought her quite ordinary, in fact, not special at all. But she'd had a talent for loving people. Her whole life had been about taking care of her friends, her home, her community, and most of all, her family.

"You're my dream," I whispered. "You and our baby. I want to go home with you. Be with you. Raise our family." I lifted my gaze to his. "I love you, Edward."

He breathed in wonder, "You do?"

"I have just one question left to ask you," I said, smiling through my tears. I took a deep breath. "Will you marry me?"

Edward staggered back. Then he gave a low shout.

"*Will* I?"

As he took me in his arms, his handsome face no longer looked thuggish or brooding or dark. Joy made him look like the boy he'd once been, like the man I'd always known he could be.

"I love you, Diana Maywood," he whispered, cradling my cheek. "I'm going to love you for the rest of my life. Starting now...."

Pulling me against his body, he kissed me hard,

until I was gasping with joy and need, clutching him to me.

"Um," I heard the mechanic's awkward mumble across the hangar, "you guys still know I'm here, right?"

We were married two weeks later in my mother's rose garden. All the people we loved were there, Mrs. MacWhirter and the rest of our closest family and friends. Our wedding was nothing fancy, just a white cake, a simple dress and a minister. No twenty-carat diamond ring this time, either. Seriously, I was afraid I'd put my eye out with that thing. Instead, we gave each other plain gold bands in the double ring ceremony.

It helps to have friends in the entertainment business. A musician friend of mine played the guitar, and a photographer friend took pictures. Madison was my bridesmaid, and Howard walked me down the aisle. As I held a simple bouquet of my mother's favorite roses, in her garden on that beautiful, bright California morning, it was almost as if she were there, too.

It was all perfect. The only guests were people we really loved. Rupert and Victoria sent their congratulations and a very nice blender.

After the ceremony, when we were officially husband and wife, we held an outdoor dinner reception beneath fairy lights. Howard and Madison openly wept, throwing rose petals as Edward and I roared off in a vintage car, before jetting off to Las Vegas for our honeymoon. We spent two lovely nights at the Hermitage, a luxurious casino resort owned by Nikos Stavrakis, a friend of Edward's, happily married himself with six children.

Our luxurious, glamorous hotel suite overlooked all the lights of the Strip, which we mostly ignored because we were too busy discovering the joys of married sex. Holy cow. I had no idea how different it would be. How it feels to possess someone's body when you also possess their heart and soul and name—and they have yours. There's nothing in the world like it.

"I'm just sorry the honeymoon has to end," I murmured as we left Las Vegas.

Edward looked at me. "Who says it does?"

"What do you mean?"

"We're both unemployed now." He lifted a dark eyebrow. "We can go anywhere you want. Rio. Tokyo. Venice. Istanbul. After all," he gave a wicked grin, lifting a dark eyebrow as he said, "we *do* have a jet...."

But there was only one place I wanted to go.

"Take me home," I said.

"Home?"

I smiled. "Where we first began."

Hannah Maywood St. Cyr was born a few weeks later in Cornwall, at a modern hospital near Penryth Hall. We named her after my mom. She's the sweetest baby, with dark hair and beautiful blue eyes, just like her father's.

The three of us like to visit California in the winter. We even bought the Malibu cottage as a vacation house. But now we've been married a year, we're already starting to outgrow it.

It's summer again, and Hannah is starting to walk. Cornwall is a sight to behold, all brilliant blue skies and fields of wildflowers. I've started a small theater company in a nearby town, just to be creative and have fun with new friends—because who doesn't love a play? But most of my time has been spent on my project of remodeling Penryth Hall, to let the light in. A dangerous endeavor. Yesterday I smashed my thumb with a hammer. I have no idea what I'm doing. But that's part of the fun.

Edward opened his new business a few months ago, manufacturing athletic gear for adventure sports like skydiving and mountain climbing, renting a old factory in Truro. It's a small company, but rapidly growing, and he loves every day of it. We live a mostly simple life. We got rid of the jet, sold the townhouse in London. Honestly, we didn't need that stuff. We took most of the payout from his St. Cyr Global shares to create a foundation to help children all over the world, whether they need families or homes, water or school or shoes. I think my mom would approve.

We aren't filthy rich anymore, but we have enough, and we're rich in the things that matter most. Love. Hope. Most of all, family.

Madison was nominated for a prestigious award for that little movie she did in Mongolia, which left her unrecognizable as a gaunt slave of Genghis Khan riding bareback across the steppes. She was thrilled, but she's even happier now she's found true love with someone totally outside the industry—a hunky fireman. "He actually *saves lives,* Diana. And he's so funny and makes this amazing lasagna...." My stepsister is a loving aunt to Hannah and often sends pictures and toys.

Madison is happy, even with all the minor annoyances of being a movie star.

Annoyances I'll never have to worry about, since my agent fired me, as threatened, when I told him I was turning down that movie after all. I called Jason next, to tell him I was leaving Hollywood to marry Edward. He got choked up, telling me in his Texas drawl that he'd never get over me, never. Then he replaced me with a beautiful blonde starlet in the five seconds it took you to read this sentence.

Howard visits our little family in England when he can, on breaks from his zombie series; or else we visit him on set, as we did recently in Louisiana where he was directing his upcoming TV Christmas movie, *Werewolves Vs. Santa.* (In case you're wondering, Santa wins.) He's just started dating a gorgeous sixty-year-old makeup artist named Deondra. After almost a decade alone, he's giddy as a teenager.

He's also the proudest grandpa alive, and the love is mutual. At just eleven months old, Hannah is already showing a scary amount of interest in covering her face in gray makeup and making "ooh—ooh" noises, just like all the zombie "friends" of her Grandpa Howard. Maybe she'll go into that particular family business. Who knows?

But here in Cornwall, it's August and the world is in bloom. As our little family sits together on a blanket, having a picnic amid the newly-tended garden behind Penryth Hall, I look down at Hannah playing next to me on the blanket, building a bridge out of blocks. Nearby, our sheepdog Caesar is rolling in the grass, snuffing with satisfaction before going back to chew a juicy bone. In the distance below the cliffs, the sun is sparkling over the Atlantic. The ocean stretches out toward the west, toward the new world, as far as the eye can see.

Our own new world is limitless and new.

I look behind me, at the gray stone hall I've come to love. The first time I saw it, it looked like a ghost castle in twilight. I thought then that it was a place to hide.

Instead, it was the place I came alive. The place where my body and soul blazed into fire. Where Edward and I each sought sanctuary when we were hurt, and Penryth Hall healed us.

It was the place our family began.

"I love you, Diana," Edward whispers now behind me. I lean back against his chest, against his legs that are wrapped around mine, as one of his large hands rests protectively over the swell of my belly. Yes, I'm pregnant again. A boy this time.

Life is more complicated than the movies, that's for sure. But it's also better than I ever dared dream. Real life, the one I'm living right now, is better than any fantasy. Smashed thumbs and all.

I've finally found the place I belong.

Mrs. Warreldy-Gribbley never wrote a "how-to" manual about how to fall in love, or raise a child, or discover what you really want in life. Because there are no guide books for that, really. There are no surefire, guaranteed instructions. Each one of us can only wake up each morning and make the best choices we can, hundreds of choices each day, big ones and little ones we don't even think about.

Sometimes bad things happen. But sometimes we get lucky. Sometimes we're brave. And sometimes, when we least expect it, we're loved more than we deserve.

It turned out I didn't need to be a movie star. I didn't need to be famous or rich. I just needed to be loved, and to be brave enough to love back with all my heart.

People can change, Howard told me once. *Sometimes for better than you can imagine.*

He was right. Real life can be better than any dream. And it's happening, right now, all around us.

* * * * *

MILLS & BOON®
Large Print – May 2015

THE SECRET HIS MISTRESS CARRIED
Lynne Graham

NINE MONTHS TO REDEEM HIM
Jennie Lucas

FONSECA'S FURY
Abby Green

THE RUSSIAN'S ULTIMATUM
Michelle Smart

TO SIN WITH THE TYCOON
Cathy Williams

THE LAST HEIR OF MONTERRATO
Andie Brock

INHERITED BY HER ENEMY
Sara Craven

TAMING THE FRENCH TYCOON
Rebecca Winters

HIS VERY CONVENIENT BRIDE
Sophie Pembroke

THE HEIR'S UNEXPECTED RETURN
Jackie Braun

THE PRINCE SHE NEVER FORGOT
Scarlet Wilson

MILLS & BOON®
Large Print – June 2015

THE REDEMPTION OF DARIUS STERNE
Carole Mortimer

THE SULTAN'S HAREM BRIDE
Annie West

PLAYING BY THE GREEK'S RULES
Sarah Morgan

INNOCENT IN HIS DIAMONDS
Maya Blake

TO WEAR HIS RING AGAIN
Chantelle Shaw

THE MAN TO BE RECKONED WITH
Tara Pammi

CLAIMED BY THE SHEIKH
Rachael Thomas

HER BROODING ITALIAN BOSS
Susan Meier

THE HEIRESS'S SECRET BABY
Jessica Gilmore

A PREGNANCY, A PARTY & A PROPOSAL
Teresa Carpenter

BEST FRIEND TO WIFE AND MOTHER?
Caroline Anderson

0515 Rom LP

MILLS & BOON®

Why shop at millsandboon.co.uk?

Each year, thousands of romance readers find their perfect read at millsandboon.co.uk. That's because we're passionate about bringing you the very best romantic fiction. Here are some of the advantages of shopping at www.millsandboon.co.uk:

* **Get new books first**—you'll be able to buy your favourite books one month before they hit the shops

* **Get exclusive discounts**—you'll also be able to buy our specially created monthly collections, with up to 50% off the RRP

* **Find your favourite authors**—latest news, interviews and new releases for all your favourite authors and series on our website, plus ideas for what to try next

* **Join in**—once you've bought your favourite books, don't forget to register with us to rate, review and join in the discussions

Visit **www.millsandboon.co.uk**
for all this and more today!